D0054911

She'd forgotten what Zack's love was like

Now Julie remembered the earth-shattering movement of his lips against hers as he slowly devoured her, drew her into him, the contours of their bodies so closely entwined she was unaware of the deep surging throb of his thighs against hers, of the trembling of his body as he held back from showing her his full passion—the emotion that frightened her so much.

It was finally this fear that made her wrench away from him.

"And what would your girlfriend think of *that*?" she scorned shakily.

"Do you intend telling her?" Zack rasped.

"No."

Zack smoothed his ruffled hair. "Then she won't think anything of it."

"You don't intend telling her?"

"No. The fact that I just kissed my wife is no one's business but my own."

CAROLE MORTIMER
is also the author of these

Harlequin Presents

These books may be available at your local bookseller.

For a free catalog listing all titles currently available,
send your name and address to:

HARLEQUIN READER SERVICE
1440 South Priest Drive, Tempe, AZ 85281
Canadian address: Stratford, Ontario N5A 6W2

CAROLE MORTIMER

love unspoken

Harlequin Books

TORONTO • NEW YORK • LONDON
AMSTERDAM • PARIS • SYDNEY • HAMBURG
STOCKHOLM • ATHENS • TOKYO • MILAN

For
John and Matthew

———————◆—◆—◆———————

Harlequin Presents first edition October 1983
ISBN 0-373-10636-X

Original hardcover edition published in 1983
by Mills & Boon Limited

Copyright © 1983 by Carole Mortimer. All rights reserved.
Philippine copyright 1983. Australian copyright 1983.
Except for use in any review, the reproduction or utilization of
this work in whole or in part in any form by any electronic,
mechanical or other means, now known or hereafter invented,
including xerography, photocopying and recording, or in any
information storage or retrieval system, is forbidden without
the permission of the publisher, Harlequin Enterprises Limited,
225 Duncan Mill Road, Don Mills, Ontario, Canada M3B 3K9.

All the characters in this book have no existence outside the
imagination of the author and have no relation whatsoever to
anyone bearing the same name or names. They are not even
distantly inspired by any individual known or unknown to the
author, and all the incidents are pure invention.

The Harlequin trademarks, consisting of the words
HARLEQUIN PRESENTS and the portrayal of a Harlequin,
are trademarks of Harlequin Enterprises Limited and are
registered in the Canada Trade Marks Office; the portrayal
of a Harlequin is registered in the United States Patent
and Trademark Office.

Printed in U.S.A.

CHAPTER ONE

THANK heavens the flight was over; the sooner she got to her flat and got some sleep the better she was going to feel. It had been a gruelling two weeks, the last three days nightmarishly so.

'It was bad, hmm?' the man at her side spoke.

She turned to look at Steve Carter, finding comfort from his untidy normality, the long dark hair, laughing blue eyes, and casual clothing. 'Yes,' she sighed. 'I really thought they were going to shoot us all.'

He took her hand in his. 'So did I,' he admitted shakily.

'Oh, Steve!' Some of Julie's own tension left her, as she saw how pale Steve was beneath his tanned skin. 'I'm fine—really.'

'I wish I could have been with you.'

She gave a rueful smile. 'And then maybe it would have been you they shot instead of Matt.'

'How is he?'

Her smile deepened. 'Complaining about the food when I last saw him.'

'It was just a shoulder wound?'

'I don't think Matt looks on it as *just* something.' She closed her eyes, reliving the moment when Matt had unwittingly antagonised the terrorists who had taken their plane hostage, seeing the blood that seemed to be everywhere as he collapsed after the angry burst of gunfire, clutching his shoulder as the blood seeped through his fingers and down his hand.

The flight had started out so boringly normal, the

long journey in front of them suddenly interrupted as
the Middle Eastern gunmen demanded the release of
their fellow terrorists all over the world. They made the
pilot return to the United States, and over the next
three days continued to make their demands. Poor Matt
had made a scathing comment to a fellow-traveller
about the respective governments never agreeing to let
those murderers free, not realising that one of the
terrorists was standing behind him.

Matt had passed out from the pain of his gun-wound
and Julie began screaming at the gunman, sure that he
had killed Matt. They had only gone to the States to
cover a campaign leading up to a Presidential election,
she as the reporter, Matt as the photographer, and she
had thought they had killed Matt. Her screaming had
stopped when the gunman hit her across the face with
his gun, and the cut and bruise were still very noticeable
on her pale cheek. Matt, luckily, had passed out from
the shock, although the blood wouldn't seem to stop
flowing. The terrorists had finally agreed to let him off
the plane so that he could get medical treatment.

Two days ago the terrorists had given up; the money
they had requested was available, but the demands for
the release of the prisoners had been flatly refused. For
Julie and a hundred other passengers the nightmare had
finally been over. Matt had been admitted to hospital,
and that was where she had seen him yesterday, his
usual ready smile back in evidence as he claimed to
have known those men would never get away with it.
Julie wished she could have had his confidence—she
had been terrified!

'I'm sorry, love,' Steve squeezed her hand now. 'I
didn't mean to upset you. Did you see the story in the
newspaper?'

As soon as the doctors had finished examining her

and she could book into a hotel she had got in touch with her editor at the *Daily Probe*, giving him the full story—from the inside. She had bought a newspaper at the airport, a photograph of herself—completely out of date—and one of Matt, accompanying the sensational story on the front page. Julie hadn't written the story herself, feeling too weary to do anything other than pass on the necessary information to Doug; she had let someone else write up the story. Unfortunately, as far as she was concerned, David Miles had gone overboard, even going as far as to guess her thoughts and fears during that terrifying forty-eight hours.

'I saw it,' she said dryly.

'You didn't like it,' Steve said knowingly.

'David makes me out to be some Simpering Sara. I was frightened, yes, but then so would he have been in my position.' Her green eyes were shadowed, her face pale beneath the golden tan.

'Anyone would,' Steve squeezed her hand. 'Oh, I wish Doug hadn't sent me off to Italy with Sean. Anyone could have filmed the Italian politicians.'

'Anyone could have interviewed and filmed the American ones too,' she derided. 'It's amazing how politicians all over the world look and talk the same.'

'Lying and cheating?'

'Something like that,' she laughed. 'I only hope this series of stories on world politics is worth Matt getting shot,' she sobered.

'That was incidental——'

'Incidental!' she interrupted angrily. 'Try telling his wife and two little boys that! Madge must have gone through hell when they gave out the information that a *Daily Probe* member of staff had been shot.'

'So did I,' he rasped. 'I thought it was you! The whole newspaper was in an uproar. And when I said

incidental I didn't mean it wasn't important, I meant that it didn't happen because of the job. It could have been anyone on that plane.'

'Yes,' Julie agreed dully.

'I still wish I could have been with you,' Steve said grimly.

The two of them more often than not worked together, and it was through this continual closeness that they had started to see each other out of working hours. The last six months they had been dating were some of the happiest Julie had ever spent.

'It's all over,' she assured him. 'I just want to get back to normal—I won't even complain the next time Doug gives me a boring story to cover,' she added teasingly.

Steve's hand moved from hers to touch the cut and bruise on her right cheek just below her eye. 'Does it hurt?' he asked concernedly.

'Not too much now,' she dismissed.

'Reporting isn't woman's work——'

Julie instantly shut out Steve's heated tirade, similar words echoing in her memory—'You aren't tough enough', 'I don't like you exposed to such pain and suffering', and finally, bitterly, 'You're so busy trying to do your job as well as a man that you've forgotten how to be a woman!' They hadn't been words Steve had spoken, but another man, a man who refused to accept compromise, especially in love.

The last taunt had been the one that hurt her the most. Her femininity now was something that was never in doubt, but then neither was her ability as one of the top reporters the *Daily Probe* had. And she had achieved this aim at the sacrifice of one man, a man who demanded complete subjugation in a relationship, a man who had refused to see her as wanting a career as well as him.

Up until today she had thought Steve lacking in chauvinism, her relationship with him was a sharing of interests and physical attraction. Steve satisfied both her intellectual and physical needs, although lately she had been aware of a growing impatience in him to deepen the latter.

She shrugged dismissively. 'As you said, the hijack was completely incidental.'

'I suppose so,' he agreed grudgingly. 'But it gave me a scare to know you were on that plane. Look, I know you want to rest now, but later on tonight, can I take you to dinner? I want to talk to you.'

Julie couldn't really look that far ahead yet, she just wanted to collapse into her own bed and sleep for a few hours. But she knew that once she had slept, dinner out would be nice. 'I'd like that,' she accepted.

Her flat was just as she remembered it, clean and bright, and totally impersonal, intentionally so. She was away so much that her home had to be wherever she happened to be at the time, and as far as she was concerned this flat was just her base whenever she happened to be in London. But today it was more than that, and its familiarity made her feel tearful.

'I used my key to stock up the fridge,' Steve murmured softly.

'Thanks.' She gave a grateful smile, although food hadn't been something she had thought of herself. She had given Steve a key to her flat after he had waited on the doorstep for her a couple of times when she had been delayed on a story, but so far he had rarely used it. She was glad that this time he had, knowing that once she got over this incredible tiredness she would start to feel hungry again.

She had picked her mail up from downstairs on her

way in, and flicked through it uninterestedly. Bills and more bills. There were a few personal letters, but most of them could wait, except the one from Connie; that one she would read as soon as she was alone.

'Shall I put this in the bedroom?' Steve gained her attention, indicating the single suitcase she had brought home with her.

'Oh—thanks.' She glanced up from her mail to smile at him, the pale wintry sunlight from the window behind her making her hair look like a deep red flame, the riotous curls resting lightly on her shoulders, kept easily in style—she just washed it and left it to dry!

To the man looking at her she was everything that was feminine, her wide green eyes fringed by dark lashes, her nose small and straight, her mouth, unsmiling now, saved from sternness by the sensuality of the fuller lower lip. Her tailored black suit showed the perfection of her slender figure, the smoothness of her long legs, and her height added to her graceful elegance.

'To hell with this!' Steve dropped the case on the floor. 'I just want to kiss you, hold you. Julie . . .' he groaned, his mouth coming down forcefully on hers as he kissed her with a hunger he didn't try to hide. 'Oh, Julie, I missed you,' he gasped. 'Let's go into the bedroom. Darling, I want to love you!'

'No!' She pulled away from him, high colour in her cheeks. 'You know how I feel about that.'

'Julie, we have to talk——'

'No now,' she groaned, looking suddenly fragile, her skin translucent. 'Please, not now, Steve.' She looked at him with pleading eyes.

'All right,' he drew in a ragged breath as he fought for control. 'But later—I have to talk to you then. I *need* to talk to you, Julie.'

She viewed the intensity of his expression with something like dismay. She knew that look too well, had seen it many times before, and she was no more willing now to commit herself body and soul to a man than she had been four years ago. At twenty-two she had met the man she had thought she would love for all time, and who claimed to love her in the same way, but it hadn't been enough, and she doubted it ever would be.

This same intensity she hadn't expected from Steve, in fact it had been his casual, almost ruthless, attitude to relationships that had first attracted her to him. His attitude had suited her, their casual way of meeting two or three evenings a week had suited her too. And now it looked as if Steve wanted to change all that.

'All right, later,' she agreed reluctantly. 'But I really do have to get some sleep now.'

'Of course!' He was instantly contrite, releasing her. 'I have to get back to work, anyway. You know Doug, he only gave me a couple of hours off to meet you.'

'Sounds like Doug,' Julie grimaced.

'This doesn't.' Steve put her suitcase in her bedroom. 'He's given you the week off.' He looked down at Julie expectantly. 'Nice, hmm?'

She laughed lightly. 'Considering it's Thursday now he's being very generous,' she taunted.

Steve laughed too. 'I didn't mean this week, I meant next week.'

She frowned. 'He's given me that off too?'

'Yes.'

'Why?'

Steve shrugged. 'You went through a nasty ordeal, you deserve a break.'

'But it isn't like Doug——'

'Orders from upstairs, I suppose. Besides,' he

grinned, 'it says in the paper that you've been given time off to recover from the hijack. They can hardly go back on such a public announcement.'

'They'll have to,' Juliet told him firmly. 'There's no way I'm going to spend a week rattling about here,' she explained. To be alone all day, every day, for a week, was not something she wanted right now. She wanted to be around people, to be assured that the danger was finally over.

Steve sighed. 'I told Doug you would say that. I even asked him if I could take a week off so that we could go away somewhere.'

'And?'

He pulled a face. 'His generosity didn't extend that far. In fact, he's sending me off to Yugoslavia first thing in the morning.'

'The political series again?'

'Mm,' he nodded. 'Yugoslavia after Tito—that's the angle.'

'Should be an interesting one.'

'The best yet,' he agreed. 'But it means I'm going to be away when you need me.'

'It can't be helped,' Julie shrugged. 'And I have no intention of staying off work. I'll go mad sitting here all day.'

'They'll probably bar the door and not let you in,' he grinned.

'I'll give Doug a call, see if I can't change his mind.'

Steve grimaced. 'You won't.'

'I can try,' she said stubbornly.

'Okay, love,' he kissed her briefly on the mouth. 'Get some rest now and I'll pick you up at eight o'clock.'

'Mario's?' she said hopefully.

'Mario's,' he agreed laughingly before leaving.

Mario's was a quiet little Italian restaurant in the back streets of London. They had gone there on their first date together, finding the relaxed atmosphere conducive to talking, and they had talked about everything and nothing until the early hours of the morning. Julie knew that its informal friendliness was all she could stand today.

Her telephone call to Doug did absolutely no good. He had decided she was to have next week off, and that was the end of the matter as far as he was concerned. Argument seemed futile, and so by the time the call came to an end she had accepted that the next week was all hers. Although she had no idea what to do with it, especially as Steve was going to be away most of that time.

She put off reading Connie's letter for as long as she could, wanting to read the letter from her childhood friend, and yet dreading any mention of Zack. But after showering and washing her hair she couldn't put it off any longer, knowing she would never sleep, no matter how tired she was, until the letter had been read.

The first couple of pages were Connie's usual chatter about Ben and the children, three-year-old Nicholas and year-old Suzanne. Mention of the latter reminded Julie that she hadn't seen the little girl for almost six months; the last two times she had met Connie it had been in town for lunch, her more than capable housekeeper taking care of the children for her.

She was beginning to think Connie wasn't going to mention Zack when suddenly she came to the paragraph about him. What she read made her blanch. Zack was going out with someone—someone called Teresa! She was nice, Connie said, and little Nicholas and Suzanne liked her, and you couldn't fool children, could you, her friend chattered on. They had been dating a few months now, and Zack seemed quite serious about her.

Oh, no! Julie crumpled the letter into a tight ball, her hands clenched in front of her as she bent her head in pain. Three years—three years since she and Zack had broken up, and yet the knowledge that he might be going to marry someone else still had the power to wound her emotionally.

It was dog-in-the-manger, she knew that. She and Zack weren't suited, had never been suited, only it had taken Zack longer to realise that than it had her, for him to accept their break-up as final. Well, he had accepted it now, was in love with a woman called Teresa. And she had Steve, so why should the fact that Zack had found someone he could be serious about bother her so much?

It shouldn't bother her, she knew it shouldn't, their lives were separate now and would remain that way. She hadn't even seen him for three years! But she could remember him, could vividly remember every detail of the man she had once loved. Tall and lean, with a boundless vitality that made him a success at everything he did. Incredibly handsome, styled dark hair, jutting brows, icy grey eyes, a long hawkish nose, sensual mouth, his jaw square and firm. Yes, Zachary Reedman had everything a woman could ever want, and they had wanted him, his wealth a bonus few women could resist. And yet he had been faithful to Julie during their year together, she had never doubted that.

He would be thirty-nine now, just, and he had always told her he intended having a wife and family by the time he was forty. Maybe this Teresa was it. Zack would make a good father, firm but fair, and it looked as if Teresa was going to be his children's mother.

She couldn't sleep now, her mind was too active, her

thoughts too disturbing. Zack had seen other women during the last three years, she knew that, just as she had seen other men, but they had been only fleeting affairs, according to Connie. This Teresa must mean something more than that for Connie to have mentioned her at all.

She jumped nervously as the telephone rang at her bedside, picking it up to automatically recite her number.

'Julie? Is that you?'

She instantly recognised Connie's voice. 'I was just reading your letter.'

'Oh, I wrote that a couple of weeks ago,' her friend dismissed. 'How are you, Julie?'

'Very well. How are you and Ben? And the family? Has Suzanne cut all her teeth yet? And how does Nicholas like nursery-school——'

'Really, Julie,' Connie cut in impatiently, 'I didn't call you to tell you about Suzanne and Nicholas. I read the newspaper this morning, and I've been so worried about you. You must be exhausted!'

'A little tired,' Julie admitted. 'I'll be okay after a week's rest.'

'That's why I'm calling, actually. Ben and I would like you to come and stay with us.'

'*Ben* and you?'

'Of course,' Connie said firmly. 'You're my best friend, Julie, it's only right you should come to us for a while.'

'I may be your friend, but Ben is Zack's brother,' Julie reminded her softly.

'It was Ben's suggestion.'

'It was?' She couldn't hide her surprise.

'Yes. Please come!'

It was very tempting—after all, Steve would be

leaving in the morning, and the next week on her own stretched in front of her. 'I—All right,' she accepted.

'Tomorrow?'

'Yes,' she agreed determinedly.

As Julie prepared for her date with Steve that evening she still wasn't sure she had done the right thing in agreeing to go to her friend's. Connie was her best friend, in fact it had been through her that Connie had first met Ben, but she wasn't sure being with them was a good idea. Ben had always reminded her of Zack, a less forceful, less dynamic Zack, but the likeness was strong enough to evoke some poignant memories.

As her evening with Steve progressed she could sense his preoccupation; his anger with her for refusing to discuss was at boiling point by the time they reached the coffee stage of their meal.

Julie stirred sugar into her coffee. 'I've agreed to stay with a friend for a few days.'

'But?' Steve prompted, sitting back in his chair, watching her with puzzled eyes.

Julie flushed. 'There is no but. Connie Reedman is an old friend——'

'Is she married to Ben Reedman, Zachary Reedman's brother?'

She frowned. 'Yes.'

'I see,' Steve sighed.

Julie licked her lips, frowning her puzzlement. 'I don't understand—what do you see?'

'Your reluctance,' he said dully. 'Do you still care for him, is that it?'

'Care for him . . .?' She swallowed hard. 'I don't know what you mean. Zachary Reedman has never meant anything to me.'

'Oh, Julie, Julie!' Steve shook his head sadly. 'Everyone in the newspaper world knows that you and he had a thing going a few years ago, that you used to live with him whenever you were in London.'

Julie had gone very white, her eyes huge, deeply green. 'Everyone knows that . . .-' she echoed dazedly.

'Oh, maybe not the newcomers, but all of us that were about at the time knew, including me.'

'Then why did you never say anything?'

He shrugged. 'What was there to say? You had an affair with the man, it went wrong. I didn't see that it was any of my business.'

She shook her head. 'Even though I've refused to sleep with you all these months?'

He nodded. 'That was your prerogative.'

'But——'

'*Do* you still care for him?'

'No,' she replied unwaveringly.

Steve's eyes were once again narrowed. 'You sound very sure.'

'I am.'

'He's a powerful man——'

'Power isn't everything,' she interrupted tautly. She knew all about Zack's power, the influence he had in the newspaper world. Hadn't she left the *Global News* because of that power, determined once their love had died to give Zack no say in her life at all? And as the owner of the *Global News* he had had plenty of that. Fortunately he had no influence with the *Daily Probe*, her career had been allowed to grow and expand as she wanted it to away from his interference. Zack hadn't believed in a woman having a career, especially as a reporter, claiming it made them hard and unfeminine, and it had been this chauvinistic view that had finally destroyed them. 'No, it isn't everything,' she repeated bitterly.

'Maybe not,' Steve agreed, having watched the

different emotions flickering across her face. 'Julie, I want to talk about us,' he clasped her hand across the table.

She licked her lips nervously, knowing she couldn't put this moment off any longer—and also knowing it could be the end of them. 'Us?' she prompted with a feeling of dread.

'Yes.' His expression was intent. 'Julie, we've been seeing each other for six months now, and we've stagnated.'

'Stagnated!' she scorned.

'Yes, we have,' he insisted. 'I'm thirty-four, Julie, hardly a boy. And you're twenty-six——'

'Hardly a girl,' she mocked.

He shot her a look of exasperation. 'Men will still be wanting you when you're sixty, and you know it.'

'Oh, I hope not,' she said, and meant it. So far men had caused all the trouble in her life. She hoped it wouldn't still be happening when she was sixty!

'Well, they will,' Steve insisted impatiently. 'But we're getting sidetracked. What I really wanted to say was that we have to either go on or stop.'

'Yes,' she sighed.

'You already knew that, didn't you?'

'Yes. But you know how I feel about affairs. I told you at the beginning——'

'Once bitten, twice shy,' he nodded.

Julie flushed. 'No, I didn't say that.'

'I guessed it. And I don't want an affair. Julie, I—I want to marry you.'

'M-marry me?'

He gave a crooked smile. 'Yes. Is it too much of a shock?'

'I—It—Yes.' She had expected an affair, but *marriage*? Steve had taken her aback completely.

'I know,' he sighed, his expression rueful. 'I'm not exactly what you envisaged as husband material. I'm not what *I* had imagined as husband material either!' he said self-derisively. 'But we're so good together, Julie, both professionally and privately.'

Julie frowned, her eyes narrowing. 'Professionally? Does that mean you would let me keep my career?'

'Of course. You're good, Julie, really good. We could be the first husband-and-wife team on the *Daily Probe*. Until the children come along, of course,' he added with a grin.

She stiffened, her expression distant. 'You want children?'

'Doesn't every man?' he shrugged.

'Yes,' she acknowledged bitterly. 'But I don't.' She shook her head.

'Maybe not now,' Steve accepted. 'You're only twenty-six, we have plenty of time——'

'You don't understand,' she cut in abruptly. 'I mean I don't want children, ever.' Her voice was cold.

'Julie . . .?'

She sighed at his hurt expression. 'Most women are maternal, I know that, but I'm not. And I never will be.'

'You could change your mind——'

'I won't,' she said with finality. 'Oh, Steve, I told you not to get emotionally involved with me. I'm not interested in the sort of marriage you want, the little woman in front of the cooker, taking the children to school, rushing home to do the housework before you get home for your dinner. My mother's sort of marriage,' she shuddered.

'Then just what the hell do you want?' He was angry now, releasing her hand to glare at her. 'You don't want an affair, you don't want marriage,' he said agitatedly. 'What do you want, Julie? You aren't in-different to physical pleasure, we both know that——'

Her mouth twisted derisively. 'Why is it men always go back to the physical?' she taunted.

'Because as far as I'm concerned it's the only way I can reach you! For Pete's sake, Julie, you have me tied up in knots. I've never met a woman like you before— you aren't interested in marriage, you aren't promiscu-ous, I just don't know what to do with you! And you can stop smiling,' he added crossly. 'I've always been in control, now I don't know what my name is half the time.'

'Poor Steve!' She ran teasing fingertips down his rigid jaw.

'Don't, Julie . . .' he groaned. 'I'm serious about this.'

'I know,' she said sadly.

'And the answer is no,' he said defeatedly.

'I——'

'No, don't answer yet, Julie,' he cut in firmly. 'Think about it while I'm away. If you don't want children then we don't have to have any. I just want you, as my wife.'

'Steve——'

'I insist you think about it, Julie. Who knows,' he gave a rueful smile, 'you might even miss me.'

'Oh, I will,' she told him without hesitation.

'That's a start. Now let's get out of here so that I can at least kiss you goodnight in privacy.'

Julie tried once more to talk to him when they reached her flat, to explain, but now that the evening was coming to an end and they were to be parted for another week or so talking was the last thing Steve wanted to do. And once he began to kiss her, to touch her, she wasn't interested in talking either.

She lay in bed later that night, knowing that Steve

was right; this heavy petting and nights spent alone was no longer enough for either of them. He had left her with obvious reluctance half an hour ago, and she still ached with unfulfilled desire, despite a cool shower.

She was a normal woman, with a natural desire to be made love to, and saying no caused her as much physical disappointment as it did Steve. He would be a tender, unselfish lover, she knew that.

But she couldn't take him as a lover, and she couldn't marry him either. She already had a husband, was married to a man she hadn't seen for three years. She was *married* to Zachary Reedman!

How shocked Steve would be if he knew the truth, if he knew that she hadn't just stayed with Zack when she was in London, that she had in fact been his wife, had been married to him for a year before that last explosive argument.

She had been loath to make the commitment to marriage in the first place, but Zack hadn't allowed her to hesitate, had bulldozed her into marrying him as surely as he had controlled the rest of their relationship. She had hated him for it, and even now she refused to think about him too deeply.

And yet in the night, as she struggled with her sleeplessness, she could have sworn she felt strong arms about her, male arms that comforted and protected, strong male arms, Zack's arms . . .

By morning she had put him out of her mind, and went out to the shops to buy toys for the children before driving out to Hampshire after lunch.

It was a pleasant drive this time of year; the motorway out to Hampshire was one of the most scenic she had ever seen, edged by forests and heather, the mood of the drivers seeming to become less aggressive

with the calm beauty that surrounded them. Julie kept
to the slow lane, keeping the speed of her MG
moderate, although she knew the small sports car was
capable of doing better. Speed and danger were not
something she wanted at the moment, wanting to stay
in the slow lane, of life, as well as the motorway.

She had spent a restless night, despite her urgent need
of sleep. The fear and tension she had lived under for
three days were still with her, refusing to be banished
despite her safety. Once or twice she had managed to
drift off to sleep only to come awake in a cold sweat,
the memory of a gun being pointed at her making her
tremble, and imaginary male arms were no comfort at
those times.

Today she was even more pale and drawn, make-up
doing nothing to conceal her pallor—or the black and
blue bruise below her eye, where the cut was at last
beginning to heal over. Despite her claim to Connie
yesterday that she felt fine she knew her friend would
only have to take one look at her to disbelieve that.
And maybe she would be right to. Shock finally seemed
to have caught up with her, leaving her cold and
shivering on a warm day, her eyes huge and haunted,
dark smudges beneath their clouded greenness.

Steve had remarked on her appearance when she had
seen him off at the airport, and she had laughed off his
concern, knowing that in his present frame of mind he
could just refuse to go to Yugoslavia if he became too
concerned about her. He had gone off happy, she had
seen to that, although she would be a liar now if she
didn't admit that the sight of Connie and Ben's house
brought a sigh of relief from her.

It was a nice house, a beautiful house, and Connie
had made sure it was a homely house. It was large for a
small family, having seven bedrooms, but Connie had

somehow managed to give it the cosy atmosphere of a country cottage. It stood back off the road in its own grounds, completely fenced in because Nicholas liked to play out in the garden.

But he wasn't in the garden today, only the elderly gardener was there, weeding the flower-beds—or replanting flowers Nicholas had dug up, Julie thought ruefully. From what she had gathered from Connie this seemed to be one of the little boy's favourite pastimes.

The golden Labrador came out to greet her, Lady gently licking her hand as she went to get her case out of the boot of the car. As with the children, it was six months since she had seen the dog, and yet Lady hadn't forgotten her, and her big brown eyes were as adoring as ever, her nose gently nuzzling.

'I see Lady's said hello,' said a light female voice.

Julie turned to find Connie coming out of the house, a young woman of her own age, with straight shoulder-length hair and laughing blue eyes. Those blue eyes darkened with concern as she looked at Julie.

'Julie!' she exclaimed.

'I know,' Julie gave a light laugh, hugging her friend, 'I look awful.'

'No——'

'Yes, I do,' she insisted without self-pity. 'But it's just lack of sleep and the bruise——'

'That's where he hit you?' Connie looked at her searchingly.

'Yes,' she nodded.

'Animal!' her friend said vehemently.

'Connie!' Julie smiled.

'Well, he is. Picking on a poor defenceless woman!'

'That poor defenceless woman was hitting him at the time,' she admitted ruefully.

'You were?' Connie said disbelievingly.

'Yes, you see——'

'Let's go inside,' Connie suggested warmly. 'We can have a cup of tea and chat before the children wake from their naps.'

Julie's eyes widened. 'They're still asleep?'

'Yes,' Connie laughed. 'Haven't you noticed how quiet it is?'

'Well . . .'

'Make the most of it,' her friend advised. 'Once they're awake there won't be a moment's peace.'

She followed Connie through into the lounge, sitting down opposite her friend. 'Where's Ben?'

'At work,' Connie grimaced. 'Zack's out of the country at the moment, so he's kept pretty busy at the office.'

Benjamin Reedman was Zack's personal assistant. He knew almost as much about the newspaper business as Zack did, and the two brothers worked well together, almost telepathically.

'Would you mind if I went upstairs and freshened up before tea?' Julie asked brightly.

'Of course,' Connie nodded instantly. 'Take all the time you want.'

Julie leant back weakly against the bathroom door once she got upstairs. She shouldn't have come here, she knew she shouldn't. Talking of Zack was second nature to Connie, she could have no idea how it upset her. And she still had the children to greet yet. Nicholas, who looked so much like Zack he could have been the son he had wanted . . .

She was calm again when she returned to the lounge, where Connie was in the process of pouring out the tea.

Her friend smiled. 'I think I hear the gentle sound of

my son coming down the stairs,' she said as a loud noise could be heard in the hallway.

Julie's heart contracted. 'I hope I didn't wake them,' she said stiffly.

'No,' her friend shook her head. 'It's two-thirty, I can more or less set my watch by them.'

At that moment the door opened and Nicholas Reedman came into the room, a boy tall for his three years, very thin, with huge grey eyes and unruly dark curls. He looked even more like Zack than when Julie had last seen him, and her breath caught in her throat. He was exactly the sort of child Zack would have liked for his own, and she felt sure he doted on his small niece and nephew, just as he would have doted on his own child . . .

The little boy eyed her warily, walking around the furniture to his mother, his gaze never leaving Julie, and he clutched his mother's dress as he reached her side.

'I thought you said he remembered me,' Julie teased abruptly.

'He does,' Connie insisted. 'Nicholas, this is Aunty Julie,' she prompted.

'Julie?' His expression brightened.

'That's right,' Julie reassured him softly. 'And I bought you a present.'

'Police car!' he exclaimed excitedly.

'No, that was last time,' she laughed. This meeting with Nicholas was going off easier than she had thought it would. After all, he wasn't the baby she remembered any more, but a sturdy little boy. It was so easy to love him. 'I've bought you something else this time.'

'Bribery and corruption!' her friend muttered as Nicholas exclaimed over the farm she had bought him.

'Maybe, but it works,' she laughed as Nicholas

hugged her, her arms tightening convulsively before she released him.

Suzanne turned out to be more like her mother, with baby blonde curls and huge blue eyes, quite grown up for just over a year old, and she loved the rotating activity centre Julie had bought for her.

'You love all this, don't you?' Julie said to her friend as the children played happily at their feet. 'Being a wife and mother,' she explained at Connie's questioning look. 'And I don't mean that disparagingly.'

'I know you don't,' Connie accepted softly. 'And yes, I love it—as much as you like working on the newspaper. You still enjoy it as much?'

'Yes.' It was her whole life, she could never imagine being without it. In fact, if it hadn't been for the anchor of her job she doubted she would have survived the trauma that had followed her break-up with Zack.

'Even after——' Connie broke off, biting her lip. 'Sorry.'

'Don't keep apologising,' Julie shook her head. 'Even after the last few days I still want to carry on reporting.'

'Is it worth it?'

'Yes,' she replied emphatically.

'We thought it was you, you know,' her friend's expression was strained. 'When they announced on the news that a reporter from the *Daily Probe* had been shot on that plane—lord, we really thought it was you!'

Julie swallowed hard. 'We?'

'All of us,' Connie nodded. 'Ben and I—and Zack. Julie——'

'I think Nicholas needs some help with his farm.' Julie got down on the carpet with the little boy, helping him put up the fences for his plastic animals. 'No more, Connie—please!'

'All right,' her friend accepted quietly.

The rest of the afternoon was spent lightheartedly as the two girls played with the children, and Julie was up in her room changing for dinner when she heard Ben's car in the driveway. At least, she presumed it was Ben, Connie hadn't mentioned expecting anyone else for dinner.

As it was already seven-thirty Suzanne was in bed, and Connie was just in the process of giving Nicholas his bath. Considering that Connie could more than have afforded to have hired a nanny for the children it was very commendable that she preferred to take care of them herself, claiming that with a housekeeper and a nanny she wouldn't have anything to do herself.

Julie could hear Ben's firm tread on the stairs, heard Nicholas's delighted giggles as his father joined them in the bathroom. She had thought the normality of a happy family life was what she needed at this time, but now she wasn't so sure, Connie and Ben's undoubted happiness together reminded her of all she was missing.

But she could have a marriage that suited her even better than theirs did; she could marry Steve, could continue with her career, could have the perfect marriage she could never have with Zack. She may not love Steve as she had once loved Zack, would probably never love Steve as she had once loved Zack, would never love *anyone* as she had loved him. But what she and Steve did have was good, and she was sure she could make him happy.

But not as happy as he deserved to be! She could never give him all of herself, never wanted to have the children he would no doubt crave in time. And yet she didn't want to lose him either. It was a muddled, tangled circle, and one that she was going to have to have sorted out by the end of this week. Steve wanted his answer then.

The lounge was deserted when she came downstairs, the green of her dress a perfect match for her eyes, the soft material hinting at the perfection beneath rather than emphasising it, the heels on her sandals making her taller than ever.

She turned with a smile as the door opened, and the smile faltered a little as she saw it was Ben. 'Er—Hello,' she said nervously, steeling herself not to be affected by his stark resemblance to Zack. He was as tall and broad as his brother, had the same dark hair that was inclined to curl, but his features were softer, not etched out of harshness, and his eyes were a warm blue, not the icy grey of Zack's. Nevertheless the resemblance was enough to disturb her, and her breathing was ragged as she waited for him to answer her.

'How are you, Julie?' he asked deeply, the blue eyes as wary as his son's had been this afternoon.

'I'm well, thank you, Ben,' she returned stiffly.

'Would you like a drink?' He moved to the extensive array of bottles on the sideboard.

'Just a sherry, please.' She sat down, perched awkwardly on the edge of her chair. She hadn't seen Ben since her break-up with Zack, and this first meeting was turning out to be more awkward than she had imagined.

'Dry,' he handed it to her.

She gave a nervy smile. 'You remembered!'

Ben sat down opposite her. 'I remember a lot of things about you, Julie,' he said softly.

She glanced at him nervously. 'Not all of it bad, I hope.'

'On the contrary,' he drawled. 'Most of it good.

And you're still as beautiful as ever.'

'Thank you,' she blushed. 'But I'm sure your new sister-in-law will be even more beautiful.'

A frown marred his brow. 'New sister-in-law?'

'I believe her name is Teresa,' she said lightly, hoping he couldn't see how talking of Zack's second wife was upsetting her.

'Connie told you about her?'

'Yes,' she confirmed huskily.

'I don't believe marriage has been mentioned . . .'

'Does it need to be?' she taunted.

Ben's eyes narrowed questioningly. 'Why should it bother you one way or the other?'

'It doesn't——'

'Oh, come on, Julie,' he mocked. 'I know you, and the thought of Zack marrying again does bother you.'

She bit her lip, taking a sip of her sherry, hoping Ben wouldn't notice the slight trembling of her hand, although she was very much afraid that he had. Ben had changed the last three years, was no longer just Zack's little brother but a compelling man in his own right. Maybe having a wife and children had done that to him, or maybe Zack had given him more responsibility, whatever the reason he was now as formidable as his brother, and just as direct.

'Ben——'

The door opened and Connie came in, looking fresh and beautiful in a brown crushed velvet dress. 'Everything all right?' she asked brightly, looking questioningly at them both.

Both Julie and Ben knew that they had been given this brief time alone together to come to terms with her visit here, and both of them went out of their way to reassure Connie that everything was fine between them—even if it wasn't strictly true.

But somehow during that weekend they fell into the old camaraderie they used to share. No one mentioned Zack's absence from their foursome, and the weekend passed pleasantly enough.

Nevertheless, Julie felt a little more relaxed once Ben was back at work during the day, enjoying her days spent with Connie and the children, always retiring early to bed and so leaving Connie and Ben some privacy during the evenings.

She needed the extra sleep anyway, finding that now that she could sleep she was finding it difficult to get up in the mornings. Her sleep was black and dreamless, blotting out the memory of her time spent on the plane, and she slept like one drugged.

It was for this reason that she refused Connie and Ben's invitation to accompany them on a dinner engagement the last evening of her stay with them.

'Oh, you must come,' Connie protested. 'It's your last evening with us, you have to come out with us at least once.'

The complaint was a valid one, she had already turned down two other invitations to accompany them when they went out, but tonight she had to be on her own; she would probably watch television for a while and then have another early night.

'I'd rather not,' she said softly. 'I have the drive back to London tomorrow.'

'You aren't exactly decrepit, Julie,' Ben mocked, adding his voice to the argument. 'And the drive to London doesn't take that long, I do it every day.'

'Of course you do,' she flushed. 'But I would really rather not go. I—I have a slight headache,' she invented, instantly feeling guilty as she saw Connie's face darken with concern.

'You should have said,' her friend came to her side.

'Have you taken anything for it?'

'I—I was just about to.' Julie studiously avoided Ben's sceptical gaze, knowing he didn't believe she had a headache at all. And he was right! Her reason for not wanting to go out tonight was much more deeply rooted than a headache.

Connie glanced at her husband. 'If Julie isn't feeling well . . .' she gave a helpless shrug.

He looked down at Julie mockingly. 'You really don't feel well enough to accompany us?' he taunted.

She looked down at her hands. 'Er—No. Besides, I can listen out for the children.'

'Mrs Pearce can do that,' he drawled.

'I—I'd rather stay here. It isn't really important that I come, is it?' Julie appealed.

Again Connie shot a rather helpless look at Ben. 'I suppose not,' she answered lamely. 'Although it would have been nice.'

'We can do it some other time,' Julie dismissed easily.

'Maybe we shouldn't go either——'

'Oh, I insist,' she sharply interrupted her friend, wanting above anything else to be alone tonight, tonight of all nights. 'After all,' she gave a jerky smile, 'I'll probably only be going to bed anyway.'

'Ben?' Connie looked over at her husband.

He shrugged. 'We can't force her.'

'Of course you can't,' Julie said brightly. 'Now you go out and have a lovely time and forget all about me.'

She finally managed to get them out of the house an hour later, breathing a sigh of relief, then she dismissed Mrs Pearce for the evening, wanting to be alone. These dark moods of depression didn't come over her very often, but when they did she knew it wasn't wise to ignore them.

When she had first started to get them she had consulted a doctor, but he seemed to think it was a perfectly normal reaction to her broken marriage, the way it had broken up, and had prescribed pills which she refused to take. Doctors seemed to prescribe tranquillisers for everything nowadays, and she had seen friends of hers become dependent on them. She never intended to become addicted to anything again, she knew that the withdrawal symptoms weren't worth it.

It was a strange way to think of your husband, as an addiction, and yet that was exactly what Zack had been for her. She had known from the start that he was wrong for her, had tried to resist total dependence, but in the end she had succumbed like any addict. And like any other addiction he had turned around one day and tried to destroy her, just as she had known that he would.

She couldn't remember, wouldn't allow herself to remember, the good times, she knew only that tonight she would need the help of the sleeping pills the doctor had given her. She had taken them only twice before, and tonight she would need them for the same reason—to forget Zack, longing for that total oblivion the pills gave her.

She had already warned Mrs Pearce to listen out for the children, although she looked in on them before she went to her own room. They were sleeping like angels, looking nothing like the little demons that plagued Connie all day. Connie had infinite patience with them, and Julie could only admire her ability to be a mother.

But much as she had come to love the two children during her week here she still had no desire to become a mother herself. Nicholas and Suzanne she could hand back whenever she wanted to, knowing that her indifference wouldn't bother them.

She quietly left the nursery to go and run her bath, finding the hot water soothing, although the blackness that was like a heavy weight refused to be pushed away.

The masculine night-shirt she wore fell down to just below her knees, and without her make-up she looked about sixteen. If only she felt that way!

The tablets, she knew from experience, would take some time to take effect, although when they did work they would knock her out for at least six hours, something she welcomed in her present mood. At the moment all her old resentment had come to the fore, and she felt angry, betrayed, almost violent as she fought off the dark memories that haunted her.

When the doorbell rang she was on her way from the bathroom, taking two steps down the stairs before freezing, staring at the tall, dark figure vaguely visible through the partly glazed door. Then a key was being placed in the lock, and Julie's breath caught in her throat as the door slowly opened.

She must have gone deathly pale as she instantly recognised the man who stood there. 'Zack . . .!' she breathed raggedly, for it really was him. He was older, grey streaks among the black thickness of his hair, more lines on his ruggedly handsome face, perhaps a little leaner too, although no less powerful, looking every one of his thirty-nine years. And yet it was definitely Zack, the man who was still her husband.

CHAPTER TWO

ZACK tersely dismissed the housekeeper as she came in answer to the ringing of the doorbell, having eyes only for Julie, light luminously grey eyes surrounded by thick dark lashes, eyes that smouldered as he looked at her, turning back the clock for both of them.

She had been newly employed at the *Global News*, fresh from working on a local newspaper in the small town she had been brought up in. She had found London a strange world after the intimacy of Sleaford, and had had no premonition of the complete change that was going to take place in her life.

From the first day she had seen Zack she had known he was a dangerous individual, but when she had gone to work on that Monday morning four years ago she hadn't dreamt she would meet such a man, hadn't known such men existed outside the pages of romance novels.

He was everything she had ever dreamt of in a man— tall, dark, and very, very handsome. It was the latter that worried her the most. She had met too many men in the past whose looks gave them a conceit she detested.

Zack had walked into the open-plan office to talk to her boss, a totally dominating personality who instantly drew attention. She had watched him as he talked to Frank Black, had seen the respect with which Frank treated him. As he walked out of the office he had caught her gaze, his brows rising as she blushingly looked away. She had hated that blush, knew that at twenty-two she should be past such things; she had thought she was until Zack had looked at her with that totally male assessment.

She had learnt later who he was—it would have been hard not to! All the female members of the staff were buzzing with the return of Zachary Reedman from his business trip abroad, the owner of the newspaper they all worked for, and a very sexy individual, according to most of the women.

She had been coming back from one of the other offices when she saw Zack again. He was coming towards her down the corridor, and she bent her head to take an unwarranted interest in the papers in her hand. Maybe if she hadn't been acting so coyly and had looked where she was going the two of them would never have met—although knowing Zack's determination perhaps they would!

As it was they had walked straight into each other, the solid wall of Zack's chest completely knocking her off her feet. She landed in an untidy heap on the floor, her papers scattered all over the corridor. Later on, when she knew him better, he teased her about the way she had 'fallen' for him, but at that moment she had been burning with indignation, mainly because she had felt a fool.

To her surprise Zack had asked her out to dinner after helping her pick up the papers, an invitation she had refused. After all, he couldn't really be serious. Why should the owner of the newspaper want to take out his most junior reporter?

That was when she first discovered Zack's persistence. For a week he had bombarded her with telephone calls, so much so that she had begun to get strange looks from the people she worked close to. It was because of this growing curiosity that she had finally agreed to meet him for a drink one evening, sure that once he discovered how ordinary she was he would quickly lose interest.

He hadn't. That first date had led to a second, the second to a third, until at the end of three weeks Julie suddenly realised they had met every evening of that time. That was when she began to panic, turning down his next two invitations on made-up excuses.

Zack hadn't been fooled for a moment, and the telephone calls started once again. She had finally given in, almost fainting with shock when Zack had asked her to marry him. All her objections—the fact that they hadn't known each other very long, their different life-styles—had been to no avail. Once again she had come up against Zack's determination, and before she was even aware of it happening she found herself standing before a registrar, with Connie as her witness, Ben as Zack's.

The only thing she had insisted on was that their marriage remain a secret for the moment, and Zack reluctantly accepted that it could be awkward for her to carry on with her career as his wife. Reluctantly he had agreed, although only on a temporary basis. Somehow it had never seemed the right time to make their marriage public, so that even now it had remained a secret between Connie and Ben, Zack and herself.

For the first six months of their marriage everything had seemed to go smoothly for them. The two of them were often away at different times, although each homecoming was like a second honeymoon. It was at the end of a month's absence on Julie's part that Zack had finally told her she had to choose, her career or him. It had been an impossible choice, and for another five months their marriage had continued in a stilted warfare.

Zack's unreasonable jealousy had caused their final confrontation. He had accused her of having an affair with the man who had accompanied her as a photographer on the month in South Africa. It had been a ludicrous accusation, and when she had told Zack so he had finally lost all control.

What had happened next she still didn't like to think about, blocking the horror of it from her mind even now.

She had found it impossible to remain at the *Global News*, although Zack had made no effort to make her leave. But seeing him walking confidently about the building and knowing their marriage was over Julie had known she couldn't stay, and she made the move to the *Daily Probe* almost immediately.

Much to her surprise Zack had never divorced her, and so officially she was still Mrs Julie Reedman, although she had never used the name. And she never would! She was no man's possession, and never would be. Zack could divorce her and marry this Teresa, could have the family he had always wanted, but she would never ever put herself in the position again where she was responsible to a man for her actions. She liked her independence, liked being free to do what she wanted when she wanted. And when the day came that she was no longer attractive to men she would still have her career, she wouldn't have become the mental cabbage her mother had before her father lost interest in her.

No man would ever make her his doormat, the woman he came home to when his mistress wasn't available, the woman who ruined her own figure giving him the children he wanted while his mistress remained beautiful for him. The sort of husband her own father had been!

*

Zack was the first one to break the spell, turning to close the door, muscle rippling beneath the superb cut of his black dinner jacket. When he looked up at her again his eyes were the cold, metallic grey that was more familiar to her, his mouth twisting sardonically as his gaze passed from the top of her head to the soles of her feet.

'I hope that's your night attire,' he drawled finally, 'and not a new fashion. I doubt if it would catch on.'

His mockery was the shock she needed to her surprise at seeing him after all this time, to remind her that this wasn't the man she had married but the man she had left. In her mind they were two totally different men, as divisible as night and day, as angel and demon. Not that Zack had ever been an angel, she thought ruefully, but he had certainly been the latter.

'Well?' he snapped abruptly, watching her with narrowed eyes. 'Don't tell me I've left you speechless?'

He had, but she wasn't going to tell him that. She walked slowly down the stairs. 'Connie and Ben——'

'Are out. I know.' His gaze was fixed on the almost healed gash on her face, the bruising almost completely gone now. 'He did this to you?' His voice was steely.

'Yes.' She frowned. 'If you knew Connie and Ben were out why did you come here?' she asked slowly.

'To see you, of course,' he replied as if talking to a stupid child. 'Will it leave a scar?'

'Only a small one,' she told him impatiently. 'Why on earth should you want to see me?'

His hand on her cheek was like an electric shock, and it took all of her willpower not to flinch away. 'Such a beautiful face to bear a scar,' he murmured softly, his warm breath moving the hair at her temple.

She had to move away, she couldn't bear him close to

her like this. 'We all bear scars, Zack,' she scorned, and moved into the lounge, knowing her striped nightshirt wasn't the most perfect clothing to be carrying out this conversation, but the thickness of the material and the length of the garment meant she was more than adequately covered. Besides, she doubted Zack intended leaping on her in an impassioned frenzy! He despised her as much as she despised him. She turned to face him. 'But not all of them are visible.'

His mouth tightened. 'And I should know,' he rasped.

'As we both should know,' she corrected pointedly. 'Now why are you here?'

He shrugged, moving to sit in one of the armchairs. 'You surely haven't forgotten what today is?'

She tensed, her hands clenching at her sides. 'Saturday, isn't it?' she avoided.

'Don't play dumb, Julie,' his mouth twisted. 'We both know you're a very intelligent lady, a very *dedicated* intelligent lady. And I'm sure you know exactly what today is.'

'I do?' she raised her eyebrows.

'Oh yes,' Zack nodded, 'you know. You should have come with Connie and Ben, Julie. I thought it only right that we should all spend the evening together, our fourth wedding anniversary, the first one we've ever spent together.' His voice hardened to anger.

She knew exactly what the day was, as he said she did; she had been fighting acknowledging it all day. The fourth anniversary of her marriage to Zack, the reason for her black depression.

It wasn't quite true that they had never spent a wedding anniversary together. On their first one they had spent the day together. In fact, it had been the unexpected call telling Julie that she had to fly to Germany in the early evening that had sparked off that last terrifying argument.

Her wedding anniversary had always been a thing of horror to her, in fact the only other two occasions she had resorted to taking the sleeping pills had been her second and third anniversaries, when all she wanted to do was sleep until it was over. This fourth one was turning out to be as traumatic as the first.

'Connie and Ben knew we were meeting you?' she said dully, wondering how they could have betrayed her in that way.

'They had no idea of the extent to which you would hate the idea,' Zack scorned hardly. 'And you do hate it, don't you, Julie?' His eyes were narrowed.

She shuddered with reaction. 'You know I do,' she muttered through stiff lips.

'Yes,' he sighed his impatience. 'Even after three years you still can't quite look me in the face, can you?'

She was afraid to, had felt his magnetic pull the moment he had stood framed in the doorway only minutes ago—and she shied away from it.

'Don't bother to answer,' he rasped. 'I can see exactly how you feel.'

Julie wished she could, her emotions were in a turmoil. Zack was still as forceful a personality as ever, she could feel that without even looking at him, and the threat he posed to her already raw emotions made her want to run away and hide. How he would laugh if he knew, what enjoyment he would derive from disturbing her in this way!

'Maybe I have something to say which will stop you looking at me as if you hate the sight of me,' he told her harshly.

'Yes?' she queried huskily.

'You can talk, then,' he scorned.

'When I want to,' she returned tightly.

If anything his expression hardened even more, a pulse beating erratically in his throat. 'Perhaps a divorce will help loosen your tongue,' he said grimly.

Even after all the talk of Zack and Teresa his mention of divorce still came as something of a jolt to Julie, and she sank slowly down into one of the armchairs. Divorce! After all these years he had finally decided to divorce her. And why not? It was a logical conclusion to the mistake they had both made.

'I expected a more joyous reaction,' he taunted. 'No cries of joy, no tears of happiness, no prayer of thanks?' he mocked.

'I——' She could feel herself slipping, could feel the cloud of blackness slowly washing over her, and knew that at last the pills were working, that oblivion had come—at a time when she didn't want it! She tried to fight it, but her lids wouldn't be opened no matter how much she tried to make them.

'Julie!' Zack's voice came through to her in harsh concern.

'I'm sorry.' Was that slurred, almost drunk-sounding voice really her own? 'So sorry.'

'Julie!' He came over to shake her, his fingers biting painfully into her arms as her head lolled forward.

'So sorry...' she slurred again before slumping forward in a drug-induced sleep.

CHAPTER THREE

IT was almost daylight when she woke up, the familiar brown and lemon curtains in Connie's guest-room telling her that she was in the bedroom she had occupied all week. She had no idea how she had got up here, although she could take a good guess. Zack had always been a strong man, and as she blinked the sleep from her foggy brain she vaguely recalled falling into his arms. It was logical to assume he had carried her up here.

Zack. Had he really arrived here last night, on the day of their fourth wedding anniversary, with talk of divorce? She knew he had, knew it, and welcomed it. They had lived apart for so long now that divorce was the only answer. She would be free at last, could finally dismiss being Zack's wife from her life, if not from her memory.

Until last night she had thought she hated him, thought that just the sight of him again would only make her hate even stronger. But seeing him again, talking to him, had shown her that she felt nothing for him, nothing at all. He was part of her past life, perhaps not a part she could look on completely objectively yet, but in time she would. She knew she would.

And what of Zack? Once he had loved her with a fierce possessiveness, a possessiveness that had frightened her. He had sworn to always love her, to protect her, and yet a year later they had been separated irrevocably, with Zack having hurt her more than any human being had the right to hurt another.

And his love had died, as she had known it finally would—his request for a divorce proved that. He was going to marry again, would have this Teresa as his wife, would have children with her, and maybe he would finally achieve the happiness he never had with her.

She jumped with alarm as a male arm curved possessively about her waist, drawing her back into the curve of a hard body, a naked body, and lips nuzzled at her throat as she tried to comprehend the fact that Zack lay beside her, close beside her, in the double bed.

She turned in the half-light of morning to find his dark head resting on the pillow next to hers. 'Zack!' she said in a fierce whisper, shaking his shoulder. 'Zack, wake up!' she ordered in a hiss.

His only answer was to move closer to her, his arm tightening about her waist, slowly moving over the curve of her breast to probe the open neckline of her nightshirt, cupping the bare breast beneath. 'Relax, darling,' he urged as even in sleep he sensed her stiffening. 'We don't have to get out of bed yet,' he murmured.

'*You*, do!' She pummelled him on the chest, seeing his eyes open in surprise before they focused on her. He looked at her blankly for a moment, a guarded look coming over his face as he realised it was her. Julie's anger and resentment grew as she accepted the fact that it hadn't even been *her* he was urging to stay in bed with him. 'I'm sorry I'm not Teresa,' she scorned. 'But I'm sure she'll be only too happy to oblige you tonight.'

Zack was wide awake now, his eyes cold, his voice equally so as he spoke. 'Let's leave Teresa out of this,' he rasped.

Julie threw back the bedclothes on her own side of the bed and got out to pull on her dressing-gown, tying the belt firmly about her waist. 'Is your girl-friend too pure and innocent to be mentioned in the same breath as me?' she jeered, to hide her momentary pain at his defence of the other girl.

His mouth tightened as he too got out of bed, unconcerned with his nakedness as he pulled on his trousers. 'Keep your damned voice down,' he told her roughly. 'You could wake the children, or Connie and Ben.'

'Connie and Ben!' Julie repeated angrily. 'How dare they let you sleep in my room?'

Zack drew himself up to his full height, pushing the bottom of his shirt into his trousers. 'They couldn't stop me sharing my own wife's bed,' he informed her arrogantly.

'Ex-wife.'

'Not yet.'

'But soon, I hope.' Her hands were thrust into her dressing-gown pockets as she fought acknowledging how he had disturbed her when she had woken up and found him naked beside her, the sight of his body as he stepped out of bed just now bringing back more sensual memories than she wanted to admit to.

His head was held at a haughty angle as he looked over at her. 'You have no objections to the divorce, then?'

'None,' she said tightly.

'You might even be thinking of marrying again yourself?'

She gave him a sharp look. 'No.'

'No?'

Julie shook her head. 'No.'

'I've been told that there's a certain Steve Carter in your life.'

Her mouth twisted. 'You weren't misinformed.'

Zack smiled without humour. 'I didn't think I was, Connie is usually reliable.'

'Connie . . .?'

'Don't worry,' he mocked. 'She's steadfastly refused to betray her friend's confidences. I don't suppose she thought the existence of Carter in your life was a secret.'

'It isn't,' Julie acknowledged tightly. After all, everyone in the newspaper world knew of her friendship with Steve.

Zack sat down in the bedroom chair, his long legs stretched out in front of him. 'You seem to have a weakness for photographers.'

The colour drained from her face. 'Not that again, Zack,' she pleaded weakly.

His mouth twisted. 'You don't want to talk about Alec Clarke?'

'There's nothing to say,' she sighed. 'There never was anything outside of your imagination.'

'It wasn't my imagination that found you in his arms,' he rasped harshly, his eyes glittering.

Julie shook her head. 'I've explained myself to you too many times to want to go through it all again.'

He gave a haughty inclination of his dark head. 'I agree. But you don't intend marrying Carter?'

'No,' she answered with certainty, having already made her decision concerning Steve's marriage proposal. There had never really been any doubt about her answer.

'Does the poor bastard know that?'

She flushed, chewing on her bottom lip. 'Not yet,' she revealed reluctantly.

'But he will,' Zack said with certainty.

'I don't wish to discuss my relationship with Steve with you,' she snapped resentfully, her mouth twisting.

'Shouldn't you be more concerned with what Teresa is going to say?'

He looked at her with narrowed eyes. 'About what?'

'About your staying here. I'm sure she must have missed you from her bed last night.'

Zack drew in an angry breath, his mouth a thin, straight line. 'You still have a tongue like a razor, don't you?' he accused.

'I haven't changed—in any respect.'

'You're wrong,' he shook his head. 'The Julie I remember would never have resorted to taking sleeping pills.'

'The Julie you knew hadn't been through what I've been through,' she told him stiffly.

'Hell!' he swore, running a hand over his eyes. 'I didn't mean to remind you of that.'

'Of what?' she tensed.

'The hijacking,' he rasped.

Her breath left her in a sigh. 'Oh—oh yes,' she agreed weakly.

'I'm sorry,' Zack told her stiltedly. 'But when I saw you collapsing as you did I just didn't know what was happening. And when I couldn't wake you up I decided to call a doctor. It wasn't until I got you up here that I saw the bottle of sleeping pills. The doctor said——'

'You called him anyway?' Julie gasped.

'I already had,' he said dryly. 'I decided to let him come anyway. I had no idea how many of those damned pills you'd taken.'

'The bottle is almost full,' she defended. 'I only took two of them.'

'So the doctor told me,' Zack nodded. 'How long have you been taking them, Julie?'

'I haven't——'

'You took them last night.'

'That was the exception,' she flushed.

'Why?'

'Why do you think?' she snapped.

Zack seemed to go pale beneath his tan, a healthy tan that seemed to point to his having been on holiday recently. 'Because of—our anniversary?' he said in a strangled voice.

She avoided looking at him. 'Yes.'

'Julie——'

She flinched away from him. 'Don't touch me! Don't ever touch me.' She looked at him with wide frightened eyes.

His hands dropped back to his side, a pulse beating jerkily at his jaw. 'Does Carter get the same reaction?'

'Steve? No, he's gentle and considerate.'

Zack's mouth tightened tauntingly. 'He doesn't sound as if he's capable of satisfying you.'

Dark colour flooded her cheeks. 'Let's leave Steve out of this.'

'As I want to leave Teresa out of it. So that just leaves you and me, Julie.'

'No!' She backed away as he came towards her. 'Stay away from me, Zack!' she ordered shrilly.

'I have stayed away,' he said grimly, grasping her shoulder. 'For three years I've stayed away from you, and now I have you right where I always wanted you— in a bedroom, in my arms,' and he pulled her up against him, savagely possessing her lips.

Julie stood like a doll in his arms, neither responding nor resisting, aware of the desperate hunger of Zack's mouth but unable to respond to his force. Then his mouth gentled on hers, tasting rather than taking, evoking rather than forcing, the gentle probing of his lips against hers meeting no opposition as her lips parted to allow him access to the moistness within, her hands moving up to entangle in the dark thickness of his hair.

She had forgotten what it was like to be loved by Zack in this way, to feel the gentleness within him rather than the savagery, to know the earth-shattering movement of his lips against hers as he slowly devoured her, drew her into him, the contours of their bodies so closely entwined that she was aware of the deep surging throb of his thighs against hers, of the slight trembling of his body as he held back from showing her his full passion, the emotion that frightened her so much.

It was finally the fear that made her wrench away from him, her breathing ragged as she wiped the feel of his lips from hers, uncaring of the way his face darkened at the action. 'And what would Teresa think of *that*?' she scorned shakily.

'Do you intend telling her?' he rasped.

'No,' she laughed tauntingly, wishing her breathing would return back to normal.

Zack smoothed his ruffled hair. 'Then she won't be thinking anything of it.'

Her mouth twisted derisively. 'You don't intend telling her either.'

'No.' He pulled on his jacket. 'The fact that I just kissed my wife is no one's business but my own.'

'And mine!'

'Granted,' he nodded distantly. 'What did you think of it?'

'I thought it was despicable, like everything you do,' her eyes flashed. 'I pity Teresa if she actually wants to be your wife.'

'Oh, she wants it.' He fastened the plain gold watch about his wrist.

'More fool her,' Julie muttered.

'It certainly isn't more fool me, not this time,' he told her grimly. 'If there has to be love only on one side in my second marriage then I prefer it this way around. I quite enjoy having someone blindly in love with me,' he added with satisfaction.

'You don't love Teresa?' Julie gasped.

'Love!' he scorned harshly. 'An overrated emotion in my estimation. I loved you, but it didn't get me anywhere. No, things are much more comfortable this way around. And I like Teresa.'

'Like her!'

'Yes! And she'll make me a good wife.'

'So would any number of the yes-women you said bored your life before you met me!'

'That's right,' he agreed heatedly. 'Maybe I've decided it's better to have a yes-woman than a woman who doesn't even know the meaning of the word!'

'Oh, I know the meaning of it, Zack, I'm just choosy who I say it to.'

'And I'm choosy who I put the question to!' He moved to the door.

'Where are you going?' Julie frowned.

'Out. For some air. I'll see you later.'

'I'm leaving this morning,' she told him abruptly.

He nodded. 'I'll see you before you go.'

'Of course. We still have the divorce to discuss.'

'Our lawyers can discuss that. There's no need for further unpleasantness between us.' He straightened his cuff. 'Do you have a lawyer?'

'No.'

'Then I suggest you get one.'

'I trust you, Zack,' she taunted. 'A simple divorce, no messy accusation, that's all I want.'

'There's the question of settlements——'

'I don't want anything from you, Zack,' Julie

interrupted sharply. 'Especially not your money.'

His mouth twisted. 'My wealth never did interest you.'

Her eyes flashed deeply green. 'I didn't marry you for your money, if that's what you mean.'

'I'm well aware of the reason you married me,' he said dryly.

She gave him a sharp look. 'You are?'

'I gave you no choice,' he shrugged. 'I wanted you, you responded to me, I persuaded you to marry me. That's all there was to it.'

Except that he had missed out the most important fact—she had loved him, and he had loved her, with an intensity that had given him jealous rages, made him suspect every man she had even spoken to. A possessive, intense love like that was not something she ever wanted or needed.

'In other words, it was destined to failure from the beginning,' she mocked.

'I——' Zack drew a controlling breath. 'I promised myself I wouldn't argue with you about our marriage.'

'Did you also promise yourself you wouldn't kiss me?'

'No,' his voice was self-derisory. 'I never make myself promises I know I'll break at the least provocation.'

'I didn't provoke——'

'You've never needed to.' He quietly left the room.

Julie went back to bed, but she knew she wouldn't be able to sleep. There was the indentation of Zack's head in the pillow next to hers, which even when she thumped it back into shape still bore the smell of the aftershave he always wore. The times she had woken in the morning with the smell of that aftershave on her own flesh!

Thinking of that reminded her of the way he had just

kissed her. Steve gave her pleasure with his kisses, excited her physically, but never with that quicksilver burst of sensuality that just the gentle, drugging movement of Zack's mouth on hers could cause.

The cold-blooded reasoning with which he considered marrying the unknown Teresa chilled her, and his lack of love for the other girl filled her with pity. It was bad enough to be the object of Zack's love, even worse to be the object of his *liking*. She couldn't believe he was really going to marry for that reason, and yet she knew he would, knew he meant to go through with this heartless marriage.

She couldn't stand lying in bed any longer, she had to get up. Perhaps one of the children would be awake, that should take her mind off Zack.

Connie was in the nursery when Julie quietly let herself in. Nicholas was already dressed in denims and a tee-shirt, Suzanne was in the process of being washed and dressed before they all went down to breakfast.

Connie looked at Julie almost guiltily, turning with Suzanne in her arms, the little girl's fingers in her mouth.

'Before you ask,' Julie said dryly, 'and I know you're going to, I was unconscious all night, and Zack left the house about an hour ago.'

'I know,' her friend said quietly. 'I saw him before he left.'

'Then you know——'

'That the two of you are talking about divorce,' Connie sighed. 'Yes, he told me.'

'And?' Julie sensed the unspoken criticism; she knew her friend too well to be deceived.

'Nicholas, go down and have your breakfast with Mrs Pearce,' she told her small son. 'Mummy and Aunty Julie will be down in a moment.'

The little boy's hunger obviously meant more to him than listening to a conversation he didn't really understand, and he went off quite happily to have his 'toast and egg'.

'You don't approve, hmm?' Julie said ruefully.

'No,' Connie didn't prevaricate, 'I think you're both making a mistake.'

'We don't.'

'Obviously. When he said he was spending the night in your room——'

'You thought we were in for the grand reunion,' Julie derided. 'I'm sorry to disappoint you, Connie, but divorce is the only thing on Zack's mind. I think he shared my bed last night because of the sleeping pills.'

'I never knew you took them,' her friend shook her head.

'I don't, normally. Yesterday was—it was a bad day for me.' Julie put a hand up to her aching temple.

'Your wedding anniversary.'

'Yes.'

'That's understandable.'

'Yes,' Julie agreed bitterly. 'Yes, it is. But not for the reason you think.'

'Oh?'

She swallowed hard. 'I can't tell you, Connie. Not even you,' she said regretfully.

'I see,' Connie bit her lip. 'I know you argued on your first anniversary——'

'We more than argued,' Julie revealed shakily. 'But that's over now, and once we're divorced maybe I can finally forget him.'

'The divorce doesn't bother you?'

She shrugged. 'I've been expecting it.' And she had. For the past three years she had looked for the official-looking envelope being pushed through her letter-box that would be the end of her marriage. She should have realised that Zack would deal with the matter much more personally, that he wouldn't shirk telling her of the final end to their marriage. 'But knowing about it means I can't stay on until after lunch trying to be polite to Zack,' she looked appealingly at Connie. 'I want to leave now, if that's all right with you.'

'Can I stop you?' her friend said dryly.

'No,' she admitted softly, looking down at her hands. 'I've enjoyed my stay here with you, but now I have to leave.'

'I understand.'

'Do you?'

'Not really,' Connie shrugged. 'But you're both old enough to know what you're doing—I think.'

Julie laughed, with relief more than humour. 'You don't sound too sure.'

'I'm not, but as long as you both are.'

'Yes.'

'Does this mean you'll be marrying Steve?' Connie frowned.

'No.' Julie shook her head firmly.

Connie squeezed her hand comfortingly. 'Come and say goodbye to Ben before you leave,' she encouraged, still carrying Suzanne, the little girl sucking contentedly on her thumb. 'Zack won't be very happy about your leaving like this, Julie. I'm sure he expected to see you when he got back.'

Her mouth twisted. 'It won't be the first time Zack has wanted something he couldn't have. And I doubt if my absence will worry him that much, it hasn't for the last three years.'

'That isn't true.'

'Isn't it?'

'No.' Connie looked undecided. 'He asked me not to

tell you, but——'

'If he asked you not to tell me then perhaps you'd better not,' Julie insisted.

'I think you should be told. He started drinking when you left him, heavily. For almost a year he didn't even go to work. Ben had to take over——'

'I don't want to hear any more, Connie,' Julie interrupted stiffly. 'This sounds private——'

'How can it be private when he's your husband?' Connie demanded angrily.

'Ex-husband.'

'He isn't,' Connie said impatiently. 'And he was in a terrible state for about a year after you separated. When he started pulling himself together we all heaved a sigh of relief——'

'When he started dating again, you mean,' Julie said bitterly.

'Julie!'

'I'm sorry, Connie, but I can't feel any sympathy for him. If he became a drunk——'

'Oh, I didn't say that!' her friend protested.

'Okay, if he drank too much then maybe he had reason to——'

'Of course he did, he had lost you!'

'I don't mean because of that,' Julie dismissed impatiently. 'Well, maybe I do,' she corrected. 'Ask yourself *why* he lost me.'

'I think we would all like to know that,' Ben said softly.

Julie turned with a start, wondering how much Ben had already heard. By the look of him, quite a lot.

'Go and give Suzanne her breakfast, darling,' he encouraged his wife. 'Julie and I will talk in my study.'

'Ben——'

'I think we should, Julie.' He held the study door open pointedly.

She took one look at his determined expression and slowly went into the room. She had sensed the added maturity and command about Ben when she had met him at the beginning of the week, now she knew the reason for it had been the necessity of running Zack's newspaper empire for a year.

'Now,' he followed her into the room, closing the door firmly behind him, 'perhaps you would like to tell me the reason you left Zack.'

Julie sat down in one of the two leather armchairs he had in here, admiring the watercolours on two of the walls, the others lined with books.

'Julie?' he prompted impatiently, coming to sit on the edge of the desk in front of her, breaking her line of vision to anything but him, unless she chose to turn her head sideways. 'I want to know.'

'Want, want, *want*!' She stood up to glare at him, once again overwhelmed by his likeness to Zack. She braced her shoulders angrily. 'Don't you Reedmans know anything clsc?' she bit out scornfully.

'You're a Reedman,' Ben reminded her quietly, completely unperturbed by her show of anger.

'I'm *me*, Julie Slater!'

'Reedman,' he corrected softly, watching the flush to her cheeks and brilliance of her eyes with a cool detachment.

Julie flushed in the face of his calm determination, seeing at a glance that he wasn't going to move until he had been told the whole story. 'The technicality of a name isn't important right now,' she dismissed. 'What is important is that you have no right to question either Zack or me about anything.'

'I'm trying to understand——'

'Understand!' she repeated furiously. 'You're probing into dangerous ground, Ben, just because you have to *understand*!'

'I'm willing to take the risk,' he told her quietly, watching her with calm blue eyes.

'Are you?' she turned on him. 'Even if it throws your precious brother into a bad light?'

'Even then,' he nodded.

'Even if I don't come out of it completely the black woman I've been painted?'

'I'm hoping you won't,' he said with quiet sincerity.

'Oh, Ben!' her shoulders slumped defeatedly. 'You'll hate me for this.'

'No.'

'Yes,' she accepted dully. 'But I can't keep it all to myself any longer.' She drew in a deep breath. 'Zack is—was—very possessive,' she began.

'Where you're concerned, yes,' Ben agreed.

She chewed on her top lip for several seconds, getting her thoughts together. 'I never wanted that sort of husband, that sort of marriage. Maybe I didn't want marriage at all, maybe an affair would have been better. Oh yes, Ben, I mean it,' she said at his sceptical look. 'I tried to tell Zack that, to convince him that I wanted a career——'

'He never stopped you working.'

'No,' she gave a bitter laugh. 'He never did that. He just suspected every man I worked with, from other reporters to the photographers who came with me to get my stories. He became convinced I was having an affair with one of them, Alec Clarke, so convinced that he wouldn't believe me when I denied it.'

'Yes?'

She swallowed hard; this delving into the past was leaving her raw. 'On the night of our first wedding anniversary I got a call from my editor—he wanted

Alec and me to fly to Germany, immediately.'

'And Zack was naturally angry at the interruption to your celebration,' Ben shrugged.

'*Unnaturally* angry,' Julie corrected, her head held high. 'So unnaturally angry that he raped me.'

'He *what*?' Ben thundered. 'It can't be called rape between a man and his wife, Julie. If he made love to you in anger——'

'He didn't!' She was shaking now, her hands trembling as she put them up to her face, the words coming out muffled between her fingers. 'He—he hit me,' she wet her dry lips. 'He threw me to the floor, and he—he raped me.' She closed her eyes, taking her hands away, looking up at him with shadowed green eyes as she raised her lids. 'Zack raped me. He hurt me physically, and he killed—he killed my love for him. Now will you leave me alone, Ben?'

CHAPTER FOUR

THE drive back to London was peaceful, the traffic at a minimum on this sleepy Sunday morning.

But Julie's head ached by the time she got back to her flat, the tension of holding back tears resulting in a throbbing pain behind her eyes.

She sat in the chair by the window at her flat, reliving the past as she stared sightlessly outside. She had never wanted to tell anyone of the physical and mental anguish Zack had put her through when he raped her, and even now she hadn't told Ben the whole story, knowing that would shock him even more.

Rape. As Ben said, it was a strange word to use between a husband and wife, but it was the only way to describe the physical abuse Zack had subjected her to that last day they had been together.

Of course he had been sorry afterwards, his remorse genuine as he begged her forgiveness. But as far as she was concerned it had been the end, the things Zack had shouted at her as he took her would stay with her always. The names, those awful names, had been untrue, but Zack's fierce jealousy about Alec had made him believe them at the time.

And he still believed them, still thought she had had other men during their year of marriage. He might have apologised for his assault on her, but he had never taken back those sick names he had called her. And later it had been too late even to take those back . . .

Ben had been speechless after her revelation, had been visibly shocked by his brother's behaviour, but

60

had made no further objections to her wanting to leave.

She shouldn't have told him; she should have kept Zack's violence to herself, as she had always promised herself she would. But just for once she had wanted someone to understand, partly, if not fully, the reason that her marriage to Zack was irrevocably over.

She stood up gratefully as the doorbell rang. Steve. He was exactly what she needed right now to cheer her up.

But it wasn't Steve who stood outside her door, but Zack, and he looked furious, white lines of tension beside his nose and mouth. 'You little bitch,' he ground out, pushing his way inside. 'You vindictive little bitch!' He turned angrily to face her.

Julie slowly closed the door, her hands shaking as she clasped them in front of her. 'I don't want you here,' she murmured. 'The divorce can be dealt with by our lawyers, you said so yourself.'

His eyes glittered dangerously, a fierce silver-grey. 'I'm not here about the divorce, although heaven knows the sooner that's over with the quicker you'll be out of my life for good!'

Her head went back at his contempt. 'The feeling is mutual, I can assure you.'

'Is it?' he rasped. 'Then why stir things up again by telling my own brother I raped you?'

She went deathly white. 'Ben . . .'

'Yes—Ben!' Zack ground out. 'My little brother has just told me exactly what he thinks of me.' His mouth twisted. 'And it wasn't pleasant.'

Julie closed her eyes, knowing how much Ben's anger must have hurt him. He had more or less brought Ben up since their parents died, and she knew how much they had always meant to each other. 'I'm sorry . . .'

'Sorry!' he scorned. 'Why, Julie, why the hell did you

have to tell him *that*?' He looked at her with agonised eyes. 'You know I hated myself for doing it, that I got down on my knees to you and begged your forgiveness.'

'And I gave it,' she nodded dully.

'You have a damned funny way of showing it!'

'He wanted to know, Zack,' she explained pleadingly. 'He's thirty-four, old enough to know the pressure that would drive a man to act the way you did.'

'And to despise me for it!'

'He doesn't despise you, Zack,' she sighed. 'Once he's thought about it for a while he'll realise that he could act the same way if he thought Connie was having an affair. If you think it will help you can always tell him you were right.'

His eyes became even icier. 'And was I?'

She sighed wearily. 'I only said you could *tell* him that, I didn't say it was the truth.'

Zack shook his head, turning away from her. 'For the last two years I've forced myself not to even think about you, let alone the men you've been seeing, going to bed with. And yet now, having seen you again, it's all coming back.' His body was rigid with tension 'All the old suspicions, the jealousy.' He spun round, searching her pale features. 'I think the reason I've always felt this way is because you never completely gave yourself to me. You always held something back.'

Julie stiffened. 'Isn't that a woman's way of remaining mysterious?' she said woodenly.

'Not with your husband. Why did you hold back, Julie?' he frowned. 'Why?'

'I didn't——'

'Oh yes, I can see it now. At the time I was too close, too involved, but now I can see it all clearly. I knew your body, I even knew your intelligent mind, but the you behind that body and mind always held back. Even when we made love——'

'There was never anything wrong with that!'

His mouth twisted. 'Not physically, no,' he agreed ruefully. 'But even then you were holding back mentally.'

'I never wanted marriage, I told you that.'

'Yes,' he sighed. 'You told me. And you were right. You're one of those women who shouldn't marry.'

Once again the doorbell rang, and this time Julie knew it had to be Steve. She had rung him from Hampshire and told him when she would be back, and she knew this had to be him.

Zack was watching her with narrowed eyes. 'Well, aren't you going to answer the door?' he drawled.

She licked her dry lips. A confrontation between Steve and Zack was the last thing she wanted.

'I should answer it, Julie,' he advised as the doorbell rang again, and settled himself in one of the armchairs. 'I wouldn't want your photographer friend to give up and go away.'

'I——'

'Answer it, Julie!'

'Zack, you won't——'

He smiled without humour. 'I'll behave myself, if that's what you mean.'

It was, but just Zack's presence here was likely to cause trouble between Steve and herself, especially as Steve believed them to have had an affair in the past.

Julie ran her hands nervously down her thighs as she opened the door, knowing that at any other time she would have been pleased to see Steve. With Zack sitting comfortably in her lounge it was a different matter.

Steve felt no such restraint, taking her into his arms to kiss her warmly on the lips, ignorant of Zack's presence. 'I've missed you,' he murmured against her lips, his arms possessive about her waist. 'Missed me?'

'Of course.' Even to her own ears her voice sounded stilted, and her smile lacked warmth. 'How did Yugoslavia go?'

'Interesting. How was your holiday?'

'I—It was nice. Did Sean get his story?'

'Yes, after a little trouble. Hey, are we going to stand out here all day?' he teased. 'Don't I get invited in?'

'Of course.' Julie moved to close the door, effectively moving out of his arms. 'Come through.'

Steve's arm went about her shoulders, gently touching her almost healed cheek as they entered the lounge. 'It looks a lot better,' he murmured. 'I'm glad about that, I wouldn't want this beautiful face marked.'

'I'm sure you speak for the majority of the male population,' Zack cut in smoothly. 'Julie is rather beautiful.'

Steve turned with a start, shock openly displayed in his face as he recognised the other man. His arm slowly dropped away from Julie's shoulders as Zack gave him a steely-eyed look. 'Mr Reedman,' he greeted him dazedly.

'Carter,' he nodded arrogantly. 'It is Carter, isn't it?'

Julie's mouth tightened angrily. Zack was trying to intimidate Steve, and for all of Steve's brash self-confidence, he was succeeding. 'Steve, this is Zachary Reedman,' she introduced them coolly. 'Mr Reedman, Steve Carter.' Her voice cooled even more as she spoke to Zack.

Steve shook hands rather warily, obviously trying to decide what the other man was doing here. 'You run a good newspaper, Mr Reedman.'

'I think so,' Zack nodded, standing now, topping Steve by at least four inches. 'I've seen your work, it's good.'

Heavens, they sounded like a mutual admiration

society! And the remarks might have been sincerely meant, but the politeness only went skin deep, on both sides. Steve was as aware of Zack's dislike as she was, and his hackles were rising because of it.

'And what do you think of Julie's work?' Steve asked softly.

Zack's eyebrows rose. 'I have always found Julie's— work of the highest standard.'

'Of course, she used to work for you.'

'Yes.' Zack sat down again, obviously having no intention of leaving just yet.

Julie sat down too, moving close to Steve as he sat next to her. They were like adversaries facing each other across the room, all of them too polite to actually come out and say what was on their minds. Except that she knew Zack had no such inhibitions. It was only a question of time—or timing? Unless she could get rid of Zack before it got to that stage.

'I heard that you were in Europe arranging the opening of a women's magazine over there?' Steve said interestedly.

'I was,' Zack nodded. 'I arrived back here on Saturday.'

So that was where he had been. So much for his concern for her!

'I flew to Italy from the States last week,' he added enigmatically.

Julie gave him a sharp look. Was it possible he had been in America when she had?

'How did it go?' Steve was genuinely interested.

Zack shrugged. 'Reasonably well. The States and England have been my two main areas of business, Europe seems the obvious next move.'

'Yes,' the other man nodded. 'I've always found the European media interesting.'

'Really?' Zack raised one dark brow.

'Yes. I think——'

'I'm sure Julie must be bored by this talk of business,' Zack cut across him smoothly.

'On the contrary,' she told him coolly as Steve flushed. 'My work has always been a great source of interest to me.'

'I remember,' he drawled.

She flushed and stood up. 'I'm afraid we'll have to be leaving, Mr Reedman. We have a luncheon appointment.'

'Really?' He didn't even move.

'Yes.' She put her hand through the crook of Steve's arm as he too stood up, taking her hint. 'And we wouldn't like to keep Steve's mother waiting. Would we, darling?' she smiled at him.

He hid his surprise very well, even managing to smile back at her. 'My mother is a stickler for punctuality,' he told Zack brightly.

To Zack's credit he didn't even bat an eyelid, but stood up to once again shake Steve's hand. 'Perhaps we'll meet again,' he murmured softly.

'I doubt it,' Julie answered dismissively. 'Steve and I like to keep our evenings together simple—a quiet meal, an occasional visit to the theatre.'

'I like those things myself,' he said deeply.

Yes, he had liked those things too, why hadn't she remembered that before she made the taunt! 'We really should be going, Steve,' she reminded him pointedly.

'Goodbye, Julie.' Zack took her hand in his, pulling her determinedly towards him.

She suffered his kiss on the cheek without making a fool of herself, although she knew that if she hadn't turned her face at the last minute his mouth would have made contact with hers. 'Goodbye, Zack,' she said huskily, the finality of the moment filling her eyes with tears.

His hand tightened momentarily on hers. 'Julie———'

'We must go.' She moved back firmly.

He drew in a deep breath, his eyes almost black. 'Yes. Goodbye.' He turned on his heel, the front door slamming a few moments later.

'Whew!' Steve whistled between his teeth. 'There goes an angry man.'

'Angry?' Julie echoed sharply.

'Frustrated, then.'

'Frustrated?' She liked that description even less.

Steve shrugged. 'There was a lot more he would have liked to say to you, but my being here stopped him.'

'Don't you believe it,' she scorned. 'Zack is perfectly capable of saying exactly what he thinks, no matter who his audience is.'

'He still loves you———'

'No,' she denied with certainty.

'Then why was he here?'

'He—he came to see his brother yesterday, and when—when I left this morning I forgot my purse,' she invented hastily. 'As he was coming back to London Zack brought it back for me.'

'Then why did you say all that rubbish about my mother? You know she lives in Scotland.'

'Yes, well—He wouldn't leave once he got here.'

'Because he still cares for you.'

She shook her head. 'He told me he's getting married soon.'

'Oh?' Steve's brows rose. 'Anyone we know?'

'Her name's Teresa—No story there, Steve,' she warned as she realised the reason for his interest.

'But Reedman is front page news.'

'No, Steve,' she insisted firmly. But he was right

about Zack being front page news—he was, and she just hoped their divorce could be kept as quiet as their marriage had been.

'Spoilsport,' he shrugged. 'Well, as you've said we're going out to lunch we might as well go. Any preferences?'

'Pub lunch?'

'Fine by me,' he nodded. 'Just one more question, Julie.'

'Yes?' she said warily.

'Does he still mean anything to you?'

She instantly shook her head, blotting out the memory of the way the two of them had kissed this morning, and her involuntary response to Zack's lovemaking. 'Nothing,' she replied abruptly.

'Sure?'

'Yes.'

Things fell back into their normal pattern during the next few weeks. Julie's relationship with Steve continued as it always had, with no further mention of the marriage proposal he had made before he went to Yugoslavia. Maybe he knew what her answer would be!

She had also heard nothing about the divorce, but she decided that was probably normal for the English legal system. She probably wouldn't hear anything for months. Although Zack had seemed in a hurry to remarry.

Well, he would just have to wait, like everyone else did! Although knowing Zack's influence he could hurry things along if he chose to.

She was glad Steve had dropped the subject of marriage, whether temporarily or permanently she didn't know, and over the next month they met whenever they were both in London, even shared an assignment in France together, covering politics after de Gaulle. They were gone a week, a hectic week that left them too weary to enjoy the sights.

The papers from Zack's lawyers still hadn't arrived when she got back, so she rang Connie, primarily to chat to her, but also to find out if Zack was possibly out of the country and that was the reason for the delay in the divorce.

Connie didn't so much as mention Zack, obviously steering clear of the subject after that disaster of a weekend. But she did invite Julie and Steve to dinner one night, something that really surprised her.

'Are you sure?' she asked uncertainly. 'Ben . . .?'

'It was his suggestion,' Connie assured her.

'It was?'

'Yes.'

Then that meant Ben believed her about the past, he would never have made any attempt to accept Steve if he didn't. 'Er—How's Zack?'

'Very well,' Connie replied warmly, telling Julie without words that Ben hadn't told her the real reason she and Zack had broken up. For that she silently thanked him; Connie adored Zack, and would have been very hurt by the truth. 'At least,' Connie amended absently, 'he was the last time we saw him. He's only been over a couple of times since that weekend when he left so abruptly.'

'Has he been away?'

'Not that I know of.' Julie could hear the shrug in Connie's voice. 'We never see him that often. And then there's Teresa . . .'

'Yes,' Julie agreed tautly. 'So when do you want Steve and me over for dinner?'

'Whenever it's convenient for you. Would next Saturday suit you both?'

'Fine,' she accepted. 'Steve and I already have a date for that night, so I know he's free.'

'Why don't you come for the weekend?' Connie invited generously.

'Well . . .'

'We would love to have you.'

'Ben said dinner,' Julie teased her friend. 'Not a weekend.'

'But you can't have a drink if you have to drive home,' Connie protested. 'Stay to lunch on Sunday and then you can leave early afternoon if you want to.'

'You're only saying that because you don't have to cook it,' Julie joked, having put on four pounds during the week she had enjoyed Mrs Pearce's cooking.

Connie laughed. 'How did you guess! So you'll stay?'

'I'll check with Steve, but I'm sure it will be okay.'

It was; in fact Steve was quite interested to be meeting Benjamin Reedman, although Julie warned him she didn't want business discussed all weekend. Steve had a habit of doing that when in the company of other newspaper people.

They went to Mario's on the Friday evening; the meal was superb as always, the atmosphere as convivial as usual, and Mario himself came over to talk to them for a while.

'Did you and Reedman ever come here together?' Steve suddenly asked.

Julie gave him a startled look. He hadn't mentioned Zack at all since meeting him at her flat, and his mention of him now came as something of a surprise to her. 'Of course not,' she protested. 'What sort of question is that?'

'A valid one, I would have thought.'

'I don't see why——'

'He's just come in,' Steve told her tautly.

'He's *what*?' she gasped, going pale.

Steve was looking in the direction of the restaurant doorway, taking a huge swallow of his after-dinner brandy. 'He just came in, with a cuddly blonde on his arm.'

Julie had to force herself not to turn around, although she felt that familiar prickling sensation down her spine that told her Zack was indeed very close.

What on earth was he doing here of all places? Mario's was a respectable enough restaurant, the food first-class, but it certainly wasn't the sort of place Zack usually frequented, despite his claim of liking to go out for quiet meals.

Besides, she and Steve had been coming here regularly for seven months now, she had been separated from Zack for over three years, and not once had she ever run into him by accident in this way. It was very odd, and she didn't like it one bit.

She liked even less Steve's description of Teresa being 'a cuddly blonde'. That was the type Zack had always dated before he met her, and the thought of seeing him on more than friendly terms with one of them gave her an uncomfortable feeling. There was a vast difference between knowing he was going to marry again, and actually seeing the girl who was to become his wife.

'He just looked over this way,' Steve muttered.

Julie picked up her handbag. 'Maybe we should leave——'

'Too late,' Steve grimaced. 'He's coming over.'

'Alone?' she questioned tautly.

'He's left his girl-friend at their table,' Steve drawled. 'Maybe I should make myself scarce too?'

'Steve!'

'Yes?'

She didn't like that reckless glitter in his eyes. If

he challenged Zack in any way he would receive his challenge back tenfold. 'Maybe you could get the bill——'

'Then you do want to be alone with him?' he said angrily.

'I——'

'Julie,' Zack greeted huskily, suddenly appearing at the side of the table. 'Carter,' his voice cooled.

'Reedman,' Steve returned with a sneer, getting noisily to his feet. 'Excuse me,' and he shot Julie a resentful glance before moving away.

Zack moved smoothly into the chair Steve had just vacated. 'All not well in the little love-nest?' he taunted, looking very dark and distinguished in a black evening suit and snowy white shirt, his very presence compelling.

'There is no love-nest,' she returned coldly, her green eyes contemptuous, her riot of red curls made to look even more vivid against the black dress she wore.

'You and Carter don't live together?'

'You know we don't,' she dismissed.

'Why don't you?'

'We prefer our independence.'

'Physical pleasure without commitment?'

She flushed. 'Something like that.'

'And do you prefer an affair to marriage?' He was completely relaxed, watching her through narrowed grey eyes. 'You always said you would.'

She forced herself to meet that look, her gaze as impersonal as his own. 'It has its benefits,' she told him distantly.

'Yes?'

'Haven't you found that to be the case?'

His mouth quirked with humour at the way she had turned the question in on him, a cleft appearing momentarily in his chin. 'No possessiveness, no responsibility to the other person, and as I've already pointed out, no commitment.'

'Exactly,' she nodded, wondering if even an affair could be that impersonal.

'And most of all no messy legal entanglement at the end of it.' His mouth twisted.

'Yes,' she answered through stiff lips. 'How is the divorce going?'

'Slowly.' He shrugged. 'It seems that when you get married in England the knot's well and truly tied.'

'How tiresome for you!' Her sarcasm was unmistakable.

'I'm in no hurry.'

'No? I thought you were.'

'Teresa is—a warm and loving woman,' he spoke slowly. 'We can wait for the legal ties.'

'Does she know you're married?'

'Of course,' he gave an inclination of his head. 'Does Carter know you are?'

'He—I have to go now.' July thankfully clutched on to the fact that Steve was now waiting for her. 'Excuse me.'

'Certainly,' Zack came round to pull back her chair for her, his hand momentarily touching her shoulder. 'Goodnight, Julie.' He strolled back to his own table, and Julie had a brief glimpse of a petite blonde woman with an exquisitely beautiful face, the smile she gave Zack as he sat down loving and warm—as he had said the woman was herself.

Yes, Teresa loved Zack, that much she could see for herself. Then why didn't it fill her with joy to find that he finally had someone who loved him as much as he had once professed to love her?

'Let's go,' Steve said roughly as she reached his side.

'Steve——'

He dragged her along beside him. 'I'm beginning to feel haunted by that man,' he muttered, opening the car door for her.

Julie slid inside, looking at him anxiously as he got in beside her. 'You've only met him twice, Steve,' she placated.

'But you haven't, have you?' He shot her a sideways glance.

She frowned. 'What do you mean?'

Steve sighed. 'Let's discuss this when we get back to your flat.'

She had never seen Steve in this mood before, she was more used to the happy-go-lucky man who was always joking and teasing. Right now he was angry, furiously so, and Zack had caused that anger.

'Would you like a coffee?' she offered nervously once they reached her home.

'No,' he answered abruptly. 'I want to know exactly what's going on.'

'Going on?' she frowned. 'I don't understand.'

'With Reedman,' he growled. 'Suddenly he's there all the time——'

'Twice,' she reminded him huskily.

'For me, yes. But how many times have you seen him? He was there that weekend you stayed at your friend's house, he was in your flat when I arrived, and now he's turned up at our restaurant——'

'Hardly ours, Steve,' she scorned. 'It is open to the public, you know.'

'Not his sort of public,' he scowled. 'And how many other times have you seen him that I don't know about?'

'None,' she gasped.

'The man acts as if he owns you!'

'He did once. Remember?' she said angrily.

'And now? Does he own you now?'

'Steve, please don't do this to us,' she pleaded.

'I'm beginning to wonder if there is an us.' He ran a weary hand through his dark hair. 'Reedman is after you. And I don't have any way of stopping him.'

'You don't have to stop him.' She touched his arm. 'I don't want him, and he certainly doesn't want me. It was only politeness that made him come over to our table tonight.'

'And was his conversation "polite"?'

She looked away. 'We talked about you actually.'

'Me?' he frowned. 'What did you say?'

'Not a lot,' she shrugged. 'You were only gone a few minutes, Steve. We couldn't say much in that time.'

He looked at her broodingly. 'Are you seeing him again?'

'Of course not.'

'Julie, do you care for me *at all*?' Steve looked at her with a desperate hunger.

'You know I do——'

'No, I don't know,' he shook his head, his expression pained. 'I could tell you were going to say no to marriage, so I dropped that. This last month I'd hoped—well, I'd hoped things might get better between us.'

'An affair, you mean,' she said dully.

'Anything! I was hoping for *anything*.' He sighed wearily. 'I can't stand this much longer, Julie. I want you, you know that. The way you avoid anything physical between us is driving me mad!'

'Steve——'

'No, don't say anything.' He moved to the door. 'I'm reacting to my jealousy of Reedman. I'll be all right tomorrow.'

'Are you sure . . .?'

'Yes.' He gently touched her cheek. 'Poor Julie, I do put you through it, don't I?'

'It's my fault,' she shook her head.

'It's no one's fault,' he assured her softly. 'I'll pick you up at seven tomorrow.'

'If you would rather not go——'

'I'm coming with you,' he insisted firmly. 'I'm certainly not losing you now. Besides, this invitation is an indication that I'm at last being accepted by your friends.'

It was certainly that, although she had no idea how Ben was going to act towards Steve. It was all right making the grand gesture of the invitation, and she had heard nothing from Connie to the contrary of them staying overnight, but it was a different matter when faced with reality. She had warned Connie that Steve had no idea of her married status, but Ben could so easily give her secret away if he were so inclined.

'You're quiet,' Steve remarked on the drive to Hampshire.

She smiled. 'Sorry.'

'Not angry with me about last night, are you? I was acting like a bloody fool.'

'Of course not,' she assured him instantly. 'You had a right to be angry. But all that's cleared up now, isn't it?'

'Reedman, you mean?'

'Yes,' she nodded, not wanting to get into a discussion about the progression of their own relationship. She had lain awake thinking about it all night, and she still didn't know what they were going to do. Perhaps in all fairness she should stop seeing Steve altogether, give him the opportunity to find someone else, someone who could give him the love he wanted. And yet she couldn't make that break, wanted his friendship if not his love.

'Yes, it's all cleared up,' Steve turned to smile at her. 'I just wasn't seeing straight last night. Of course it was a coincidence Reedman turning up at Mario's. He had his fiancée with him——'

'Was she wearing a ring?' Her voice was sharp.

'Not that I noticed,' he shrugged. 'But you said he's getting married, so I assumed that was her.'

'I think it was,' she nodded.

'Well, if he's after you he would hardly chase you in front of his future wife, now would he?'

'No.' But she wasn't so sure Zack's presence at Mario's had been a coincidence. She had a nagging feeling in the back of her mind that he had known she was going to be there. The feeling had persisted during the night, and was still with her. Zack had shown no surprise at finding her there with Steve, had more or less come straight over to their table. No, she didn't trust Zack's motives at all.

Connie opened the door to them herself, looking very beautiful in a midnight blue dress that matched the colour of her eyes. 'Julie!' her face lit up with pleasure as she hugged her. 'And you must be Steve,' she turned to greet him warmly. 'You didn't exaggerate, Julie,' she teased. 'He is gorgeous!'

'Tell me more,' he grinned.

'Connie!' she warned.

'I think I'm going to like you,' Steve smiled at Connie. 'Maybe you could tell me later, when Julie's not around, what else she says about me?'

Connie laughed. 'I wouldn't want to inflate your ego that much.'

Julie frowned as she watched her friend. She was acting the perfect hostess, giving their coats to the housekeeper, making sure their cases were taken upstairs, the bright smile never far from her lips, and yet Julie could sense the strain about her, her gaiety brittle, fine lines beside her eyes and mouth. Connie was worried about something, she could see that.

Maybe Ben had changed his mind about their being here? But surely if that were it Connie would have let her know. Then what was it?

'Connie . . .?'

Her friend chewed worriedly on her bottom lip. 'I—er—Someone turned up unexpectedly——'

'Me,' said a quietly mocking voice from behind them.

Julie could feel Steve tense at her side as they turned to face Zack. Her breath caught in her throat at how magnificent he looked in the black dinner suit. He wasn't dressed any differently from Steve, the suit was more expensively cut probably, and yet he looked so much more distinguished, so completely dominating.

'Isn't this a nice surprise?' he drawled tauntingly.

'Er—let's go through to the lounge,' Connie suggested jerkily.

'Yes, why don't we,' Zack agreed softly.

'I'm so sorry,' Connie muttered before following Zack through to the other room.

'So am I,' Steve muttered, looking accusingly at Julie. 'Did you know he was going to be here?'

'How could I?'

'Quite easily, if you arranged last night to meet here,' he said grimly.

'Well, we didn't,' she sighed. 'Now shall we join the others?'

'Why not?' he said bitterly, that reckless look back in his eyes.

Julie almost came to a halt as they entered the lounge and saw the woman sitting on the arm of Zack's chair. Teresa!

Zack and Ben both stood up as she walked into the room, Zack's expression mocking, Ben's pleading. Poor Connie and Ben, they had had no idea Zack was going to turn up here with Teresa. Well, she wasn't going to make things more awkward for them than they already were. If Zack behaved himself the evening could still pass off smoothly. Although looking at that mocking glint in his eyes she didn't think there was much chance of that!

He put out a hand to help Teresa to her feet, making the introductions. 'Teresa Barr. This is Julie, and her boy-friend Steve Carter.'

She had been right last night in thinking Teresa was beautiful—she was. Standing only as high as Zack's chin in her high heels she had what some men would call 'the figure of a pocket Venus', small and dainty, with hair like spun gold, the latter long and silky down her back. The black dress she wore emphasised her voluptuous figure, and she leant softly against Zack as his arm came about her waist to hold her at his side.

Julie saw the gesture of possessiveness, and deliberately kept her expression bland. It didn't bother her in the least that Zack was here with his girl-friend!

Teresa was frowning now, her features small and doll-like. 'Julie?' she queried in a puzzled voice.

At least three people in the room stopped breathing, although Julie could see Zack was perfectly in control, and Steve lived in ignorance of the significance of that one little question.

Teresa looked up at Zack now. 'Darling, is this——'

'My wife?' he finished coolly. 'Yes, Julie is my wife.'

Why didn't she faint, do something, anything, to escape the bombshell Zack had just deliberately dropped? Connie and Ben looked horrified, Teresa looked uncomfortable, and Steve looked completely stunned. And through it all Zack continued to look at her calmly, challengingly!

CHAPTER FIVE

How she got through the rest of the evening she never knew. Steve's behaviour was quiet and sulky, Teresa's somewhat embarrassed and uncomfortable, Connie and Ben were doing their best to keep a flagging conversation going. Only Zack seemed unconcerned, talking quite cheerfully, caring nothing for the fact that he received only Connie and Ben's attention.

After dinner was no better, although once again Zack seemed immune to the tension surrounding him, chatting amiably about world affairs and drawing a moody Steve into a conversation about the European media.

Poor Steve! The shock on his face when Zack had said she was his wife—although to his credit he had quickly masked the emotion, and although he must be eaten up with anger at her he gave no indication that the marriage was news to him.

But Zack knew damn well it was, he had gone out of his way to find out if Steve knew they were married! Steve's claim that these meetings with Zack weren't coincidental suddenly seemed a real possibility, and Julie wondered warily at his reason for wanting to cause trouble between herself and Steve.

Because he was causing trouble, and he knew he was. His pleasant attitude wasn't fooling her for a moment, and the glitter of satisfaction in his eyes told her that whatever he was up to he was succeeding.

And he was drinking steadily, something she had

never known him to do, despite Connie's claim that he had begun to drink after their break-up. But he had been drinking wine with his meal, brandy afterwards, and now he was sipping liberally at large whiskies. She soon found out the reason for that!

'Would you mind if Teresa and I stayed the night?' he suddenly asked Connie.

'I——'

'Only I think I'm probably over the limit,' he added with one of his charming smiles. 'And Teresa doesn't drive at all.'

Connie looked awkwardly at Julie, seeing the panic in her face. 'Well, I——'

'Don't you have the room?' he persisted.

'Of course we have the room,' Connie denied instantly. 'And you know you're quite welcome to stay, both you and Teresa.'

'Maybe Steve and I should be the ones to leave,' Julie said instantly, imagining nothing worse than having to get through a morning and lunch in this awkward atmosphere too.

'Oh no, Julie,' Connie looked at her pleadingly. 'I've promised the children they'll see you in the morning. Nicholas has talked of nothing else all day.'

'And you should never disappoint a child,' Zack drawled, watching Julie intently over the rim of his glass.

She flushed, meeting the mockery of his gaze. The only child here at the moment was him, and she had no idea what game he was playing! 'I have no intention of disappointing Nicholas,' she said distantly. 'I'm feeling tired, Connie, would you mind if I went to my room?'

'Of course,' Connie agreed instantly, standing up. 'I'll come with you, I have to tell Mrs Pearce to prepare the other two rooms.'

'Steve?' Julie looked at him anxiously. He had been drinking as much as Zack, although he looked much worse for it, a high flush to his cheeks, a glazed look to his eyes.

'I'll be up in a minute,' he mumbled, taking another swallow of his whisky.

Connie looked at him worriedly. 'I've put you in the room next to Julie.'

'And will you put Teresa and me in adjoining rooms too?' Zack taunted.

'Zack——'

'Sorry,' he muttered at his brother's angry protest. 'Sorry, Connie.'

'That's all right.' She bit her lip, obviously unnerved by the strangeness of this situation. 'Julie?'

Julie followed her friend thankfully out of the room, although she wished Steve had come with her. She couldn't help feeling as if she had left him to the wolves, although that was silly; Ben and Teresa weren't antagonistic, in fact Teresa hadn't had two words to say all evening.

She couldn't help liking the other girl, which was rather strange considering their situation. But she had found Teresa Barr to be as nice as Connie said she was, although a little on the shy side, and obviously deeply in love with Zack. And there lay the trouble as far as she could see. Zack certainly didn't love Teresa. He treated her with amused indulgence while she could only look on adoringly, and Julie could see that he would be bored with such a wife within six months.

As he had been bored with her? No, never bored. There had never been boredom between them—love, hate, but never ever boredom.

But there would have been eventually, she knew that.

It wasn't in a man's nature to be faithful to one woman; she had learnt that from a master.

'Whew!' Connie heaved a sigh of relief as she closed the lounge door behind them. 'What a disaster of an evening!'

Julie grimaced. 'I can't disagree with that.'

'I'm so sorry,' Connie pulled a face. 'I had no idea Zack and Teresa were going to turn up in that way. He didn't say anything about it when he called this morning——'

'Zack telephoned this morning?' she said sharply.

'Mm, just for a chat.' Connie led the way upstairs. 'He didn't say anything about coming here tonight.'

'No, he wouldn't have done,' Julie said dully, remembering another time when Zack had forced his personality on her in this way, that time with telephone calls. He was definitely up to something— but what?

Connie turned to look at her. 'You don't sound surprised.'

'Somehow I'm not.' Julie followed her friend into the bedroom. 'Zack's playing a little game no one else understands. When he's ready to he'll let us know what it is.'

Connie sat down on the bed. 'Do you think it could have anything to do with the divorce?'

'I don't know,' Julie shrugged. 'I've already agreed to it, I don't see what else I can do.'

'Neither do I.' Her friend stood wearily to her feet. 'I'd better go and arrange their rooms.'

'Are "rooms" necessary?' Julie taunted.

'They are here,' Connie nodded. 'What Zack does in London is his affair, here he abides by our rules.'

'You never used to be such a prude,' she teased,

remembering the night Connie and Ben had spent at their flat, together, before they were married.

'Put it down to old age! Now I really had better go and sort out their rooms. What a night!' and Connie left the room with a disgusted grimace.

What a night indeed! And it hadn't ended yet. She had washed and changed into her nightgown, a flowing silky green affair, when the knock sounded softly on her bedroom door.

'Yes?' she queried in a whisper, aware that everyone had come up to bed about five minutes ago.

'It's Steve. Let me in,' he muttered.

She quickly opened the door, closing it again as he pushed inside without being asked. He was angry, furiously so, and in the circumstances he had a right to be.

'Just when did you intend telling me that little gem?' he didn't waste any time.

'Steve——'

'You're actually *married* to that man,' he accused. 'Married to Zachary Reedman!'

'It was years ago——'

'You're still married to him!'

'Not for much longer, we're getting a divorce.'

'Dear heaven, Julie, why couldn't you have told me?' He sat down on the bed with a groan, burying his face in his hands. 'Everyone thought you'd had an affair with him, but you and he were actually married! Why the secrecy, Julie? Didn't the great Zachary Reedman want it known he was married to a mere reporter?'

'It was my idea,' she choked. 'Mine and mine alone. Zack never liked it. But I—I thought it might hinder my career——'

'Hinder it?' he scorned. 'I should think it would have done the opposite!'

'I never wanted Zack's reflected glory!'

'Well, I just—I can't—How could you let me find out that way?' he looked at her accusingly. 'No wonder you didn't want to marry me—you were already married to him!'

'I told you, we're getting a divorce.'

'And is that supposed to make me feel better?' he rasped angrily.

'Steve, I'm so sorry.'

'So am I. I loved you, you know.'

'Loved . . .?'

'Yes,' he gave a derisive laugh. 'But now I know that you cared nothing for me. You didn't even trust me enough to tell me you're married. I feel betrayed, Julie.'

'I only ever wanted friendship, Steve,' she said chokingly. 'I told you that in the beginning.'

'And I complicated it by mentioning love and marriage,' he sighed.

'Yes,' she admitted huskily.

'Does Reedman want you back?'

'No,' she answered with certainty.

'Then what's he playing at?'

'I wish I knew,' she sighed. 'I thought the divorce was all settled.'

'So he can marry the anaemic Teresa?'

'She isn't anaemic. She's very——'

'Malleable,' Steve substituted mockingly.

'Maybe,' she agreed grudgingly. 'But she loves Zack, and she seems to suit him.'

'She would suit any man who wanted a beautiful doll to grace his home and bed. No man could want a woman like that after knowing you, Julie.'

She flushed. 'I don't think you're being quite fair to her.'

'On the contrary, I'm being generous. I'm taking for granted the fact that she's good in bed. I'm sure

Reedman is?' he quirked a questioning eyebrow.

'Steve——'

'Don't bother to answer,' he sighed. 'I can see he is. When I sober up maybe we should talk properly.'

'Do we have anything left to say?'

'Not a lot,' he shook his head. 'But I'm not sure if I've been offensive. I have a premature headache from the hangover I'm going to have in the morning, and I may have said things I shouldn't. I don't want us to part badly. You do see why I can't go out with you any more?'

Yes, she saw. 'I really am sorry, Steve.'

'I know,' he nodded, moving to the door.

'Steve!'

'Mm?' he turned in the doorway.

Julie ran over and kissed him lightly on the mouth, moving back as he instinctively deepened the kiss to passion.

'Habit,' he muttered apologetically before going into the room next door.

'How touching,' drawled a deeply sarcastic voice. 'And does he sneak back into your room an hour later when everyone else is asleep?'

Her head had gone back at the first sound of Zack's mocking voice. 'Is that how you and Teresa arrange things?' she snapped.

'No,' he shook his head. 'I respect Connie's wish that I don't share my girl-friend's bed while I'm in her house.'

'How noble of you!' she taunted.

'But I'm sure even she couldn't object to my sharing my wife's bed.' He moved threateningly towards her.

Julie's eyes widened as she took in the implication of his words, and she shut the door to keep him out, her heart hammering wildly in her chest.

'Oh no, you don't!' Zack put a foot inside the door and gave it a heavy push, the force of it opening sending Julie staggering across the room. Zack closed the door behind him as he came towards her.

'No!' her eyes were wide with fear, the black of the pupil almost obliterating the green of the iris. 'No, Zack, not again!' she pleaded chokingly.

His mouth twisted. 'It won't be rape this time, Julie. Not rape,' he murmured as he trapped her against the wall, moving his body insinuatingly against hers before he bent his head to claim her mouth.

She wrenched away from him. 'I'll hate you for this,' her eyes shot venom at him. 'Hate you!'

'No hate, not this time,' he promised huskily. 'Only love, Julie. Love like it used to be between us.'

'According to you even that wasn't very good,' she was desperately trying to free herself, but Zack had no intention of releasing her.

'It's all I've got,' he groaned. 'All you've got. And I intend taking it.'

He lifted her up in his arms and carried her over to the bed, coming down to lie on top of her, his mouth parting hers with a hunger that left her gasping.

'Zack, please, no . . .' she cried against his shoulder.

'Julie, please, yes . . .!' he groaned, his lips moving down her throat, lingering above her fast beating heart before moving lower, slipping the strap of her nightgown from her shoulder as he captured the tip of one breast between pleasure-giving lips, loving the nipple to full throbbing life.

Her fingers dug convulsively into his shoulder, as she heard his groan of pleasure and felt his firm flesh beneath her hands, his skin warm through the material of his shirt. His jacket had been discarded before he came into the room, his tie too, and several of the buttons on his shirt were undone. Her fingers moved impatiently to undo the rest, unable to stop herself, the skin below burning her with its heat.

'Julie!' His mouth came back to hers, meeting in a love ritual of equal desire, and Zack's thighs surged into hers as he throbbed with passion. 'It's been so long,' he groaned. 'Too long. I want to be patient, to take my time, but I—Oh, I need to take you now, Julie. Later I—We'll take it slower. But this time I can't—I need—Oh, I need you naked beneath me!'

All the time he was talking he was ripping his clothes off, first his shirt, then his trousers and dark underpants, and now it was the turn of her nightgown, and he gazed down at her with fevered eyes as she lay beside him.

'Your breasts are fuller than I remember,' he muttered, touching each rosy peak wonderingly. 'And your hips are slimmer. But otherwise—otherwise you're still the same, still the woman who drives me to a frenzy.'

And he still had the most magnificent body she had ever seen, lean and powerfully muscled, beautifully male, his flesh firm and smooth as she caressed him.

As his body joined with hers she gave a gasp of uncontrollable passion, hearing that gasp echoed in Zack as they moved together, driven on to reach the peak of physical pleasure, a release they both needed.

From the first touch of Zack's hands and lips Julie had no thoughts other than of him; she was perfectly attuned to his wants and needs, giving him pleasure as only she knew how.

It was nothing like the last time they had been together, nothing like the humiliation she had suffered at his hands, in fact she couldn't even remember that pain as Zack raised her to the heights with him, clinging to him in tense excitement as the delicious ache became a roar, rivulets of pleasure cascading down them, their bodies shuddering to earth slowly, oh, so slowly.

Zack breathed raggedly into her throat, holding her tightly beneath him as she would have moved away. 'No,' he raised his head, the glaze of passion still in his eyes. 'Stay where you are. And soon, very soon,' his voice became husky, 'I'll give you that slow loving I promised I would.'

She could already feel desire ebbing back into his body. It had always been like this between them, always this fiery passion that never seemed to lessen no matter how much they made love.

'I didn't hurt you?' He looked down at her anxiously.

'No,' her voice was thick with emotion.

'I didn't mean to rush it, but—Oh, I have to kiss you again,' he groaned.

With kisses came renewed passion, only this time Zack was determined to give her unending pleasure, his caresses slow and languorous, never quite taking her over the edge, not until they were both ready.

Julie remembered other nights when they had made love until morning, and they hadn't forgotten a thing about each other's bodies, their movements sure and erotic, finding pleasure-giving zones as if by instinct.

Finally towards dawn she drifted off to sleep, satiated with the passion of Zack's body, exhausted with a lovemaking that knew no barriers, every inch of her body knowing the touch of Zack's hands and the feel of his lips.

She woke up alone, only the indentation of the pillow beside her to show her Zack had been there at all—and the languor of her body, stretching with a feline satisfaction.

She had no explanations for last night, not for herself or anyone else. It had happened and she had no idea why. Zack had seemed as dazed by it as she was, driven on by a fevered desire that he had no control over.

Where would they go from here? Did she want them to go anywhere? She wasn't even sure of that.

There were several bruises on her body, she discovered when she got out of bed, dark marks on her arms and legs, but they had not been given in anger, only in passion. Nevertheless, they looked damning, and she hurried to the bathroom to wash and dress before anyone saw her.

It wasn't until she was trying to brush her red curls into some sort of order that she realised it was after eleven o'clock. What must everyone think of her! And why hadn't someone come in and woken her before now?

She looked different this morning. Much as she tried to ignore it, a glowingly alive woman was reflected back at her in the mirror, the green eyes shone, the features were softer, a smile curved the lips. She looked exactly what she was, a woman who had been made love to until the early hours of the morning. And she couldn't go downstairs looking like this!

Finally she had no choice. The minutes were ticking by, and she had no idea what Steve had been doing all this time, left to his own devices and Zack's biting sarcasm.

Only Ben and Steve were in the lounge when she went in a few minutes later. The two men seemed on quite friendly terms, their conversation, of course, about newspapers.

'Connie's in the kitchen supervising the children's snack,' Ben told her.

Julie glanced nervously at Steve, finding him looking broodingly back at her. She instantly felt selfconscious, as if it were emblazoned on her that she had spent a night of unbridled passion with her husband. Steve's room was next door, maybe he had heard— No, after that first exchange of heated words she and Zack had been silent lovers, moving instinctively in their desire for each other.

She licked her lips nervously. 'And—er—Zack and Teresa?'

'Gone.'

She looked sharply at Ben. 'Gone . . .?'

'Mm, they left about ten. They were having lunch with Teresa's mother and father.'

'I see. I—I'll just go through and say hello to Connie.' Julie hurriedly left the room, leaning weakly against the wall outside.

Zack had gone, had left with his future wife as if nothing had happened last night! He was just carrying on with his life as if that explosion of the senses had never happened between them.

But what had she expected, what had she wanted? She hadn't known what to do about last night, and now Zack had decided for her. She would forget it. She had been a one-off thing for him, a last night with the wife he was divorcing.

She hadn't expected anything from him, hadn't wanted anything, but this cruel rejection of their lovemaking hurt her more than she cared to probe.

She was composed when she entered the kitchen minutes later, only the paleness of her cheeks giving away the fact that she didn't really feel as bright as her mood of forced gaiety seemed to indicate.

She kept up that mood through lunch, chatting lightly about unimportant subjects, aware that Connie and Ben gave her several worried glances, although Steve seemed too wrapped up in his own thoughts to notice her brittle manner.

Poor Steve, he looked so unhappy. And she had done this to him.

Most of all she couldn't bear the shame she attached to last night. Zack had met little resistance from her, had soon reduced her to a willing partner in his lovemaking. How he must despise her for her weakness!

How she despised herself!

'Just how rude to you was I last night?' Steve asked on the drive back to London later that afternoon.

'You weren't rude at all.' Julie bit her lip. 'I thought you handled it very well.'

'I got drunk,' he grimaced. 'Something I haven't done since I was a teenager.'

'I'm sorry.'

'Did I make a fool of myself?'

'No,' she shook her head firmly. 'You were angry with me, but then you had a right to be.'

'Yes,' he sighed. 'I still can't get over it, you and Reedman married.'

'I'm rather surprised by it myself,' she admitted ruefully.

'Is he the one who put you off marriage?'

'No,' she shook her head. 'That was—It happened years ago, before I met Zack.'

'You haven't been very lucky in the men you've loved, have you?'

'No,' she rasped. 'Not lucky at all. Steve, I—Do you think we'll be able to work together—after this?' She was wondering if in all fairness to him she shouldn't leave the *Daily Probe*.

His mouth twisted. 'Work isn't everything, Julie,' he derided.

'It is to me,' she said stiffly. 'I've made it so.'

'Work can't be your lover, Julie. Only a flesh and blood man can be that.'

'And if I don't want a lover?' she flashed, last night too vivid in her mind for her to answer coolly.

'You're a beautiful woman,' Steve told her softly. 'A warm, vibrantly alive woman.'

'And I need a man?' she scorned.

He shrugged. 'I think so. And not just any man,' he added softly.

'I don't know what you mean.' She stared woodenly in front of her.

'Don't you?' he derided.

'No,' she snapped abruptly.

'If you say so,' he drawled. 'And I can't see any reason why we shouldn't continue working together. We're both adults, and we always knew it could come to this one day.'

'Yes.'

'Friends?'

She blinked back the tears as she looked at him, putting her hand into the one he held out to her. 'Friends,' she agreed huskily. 'You really are very nice, Steve.'

'Aren't I?' he grinned.

'And conceited,' she added teasingly.

They talked more easily for the rest of the journey, and Julie thought that one day they just might be friends. Things would be strained between them at first, tentative, but she had no doubt of Steve's sincerity in wanting friendship between them.

As long as she could forget that he knew her secret, had guessed the innermost secret she was almost afraid to admit to herself. Steve had known, had somehow guessed.

She still loved Zack!

She didn't want to, she had no idea why it should be so, not after all that happened between them, but she was still in love with Zack. And he had treated her as being no more important than the other women who fleetingly shared his bed.

CHAPTER SIX

WHAT was the saying, 'Life has to go on'? Well, it went on, quite normally in fact—her job as a reporter, her casual friends, her occasional chats on the telephone with Connie. Yes, life went on, but never as it had been before.

Julie had lost the tranquil peace she had known since leaving Zack, no longer felt relief at not seeing him; her misery was a tangible thing. Even her boss commented on it.

'You're not your usual efficient self, Julie.' Doug came to sit on the side of her desk. 'You've spelt Marriott at least three different ways in this story on the fire in the block of flats.'

She skimmed through the story, making the necessary changes. 'Sorry,' she grimaced. 'I guess my mind was elsewhere.'

'Mm,' he nodded. 'It has been a lot lately.'

'My work——'

'Is fine,' he held up his hands defensively. 'Even if you only worked at half capacity your work would still be superior to most of the other reporters' here,' he gave her a rare compliment. 'I'm making no complaints about your work. You just aren't your usual—lively self.'

'I've felt tired lately.'

'Maybe you should see a doctor,' Doug frowned his concern. 'After all, you went through a harrowing experience five weeks ago.'

If she saw a doctor he would just tell her to get more

sleep. And it wasn't that she didn't go to bed early—she had nothing else to do!—she just couldn't sleep when she got there.

'I just have a cold coming on,' she excused.

'For a whole month?' Doug derided.

A month, was that all it was? It seemed more like a year. Heavens, was the whole of the rest of her life going to drag in the same way?

'I'm sure it's nothing serious,' she gave a nervy smile. 'Maybe I just need a holiday.'

'You've just had one,' he reminded her dryly.

Her smile deepened to genuine humour. 'I meant a holiday in the sun.'

Doug quirked an eyebrow at her. 'How about a day in sunny Blackpool instead?'

'Blackpool!' she said disgustedly.

'Human interest story,' Doug mocked; he was a hardened newspaperman of indiscriminate years, his brown hair sparse now, his body thin rather than just lean, filled with a nervous energy that left younger men standing. 'How Sammy the cat survived three weeks bricked up in an old fireplace.'

'Oh, Doug, no!'

'Oh, Julie, yes,' he chuckled, putting the details down on her desk. 'It will be a nice break for you after all the serious stuff I've been giving you lately. Besides, the drive will be good for you.'

'Photographs?' she said resignedly.

'I'm sending Sharon with you. Two young girls should be able to charm the little old lady who owns Sammy. Maybe you'll even charm Sammy. I hear the man from the *Mirror* nearly got his hand scratched off.'

Julie stood up to get her coat. 'Sammy's probably feeling hungry after all that time being bricked up,' she grinned.

'Probably,' Doug grinned back. 'You know why I'm not sending Steve with you?' he sobered.

She made a great show of pulling on her jacket. 'He turned it down in disgust?'

'I didn't offer it to him,' he shook his head.

'Maybe that's as well,' she mocked the necessity of such a story.

'Is he the reason you look like death?'

'Thanks!' Her mouth twisted. 'And why should Steve be the reason I look like anything?'

'The two of you were close——'

'We were friends,' she insisted.

'Not lovers?'

'Doug!'

He shrugged. 'Okay, so it's none of my business. But have pity on an old man trying to keep up with the relationships of his staff.'

'My heart bleeds for you,' Julie taunted. 'And Steve and I don't expect any favours.'

'You aren't getting any. Oh, go and talk to Mrs Tibbles before I lose my temper,' he dismissed impatiently.

'Mrs Tibbles?' she laughed. 'That isn't really her name?'

His mouth quirked. 'It is.'

'I'll have a field day,' Julie chuckled.

She met up with Sharon on the way out. She had worked with the other girl often in the past and found her work excellent; the two of them were of similar age and tastes.

'I've never been to Blackpool,' Sharon smiled, settling herself into Julie's car.

'Neither have I,' Julie turned to grimace. 'But I don't think we're missing much.'

As it happened, Mrs Tibbles didn't live in Blackpool

Harlequin reaches
into the hearts and minds
of women across America
to bring you

Harlequin American Romance.

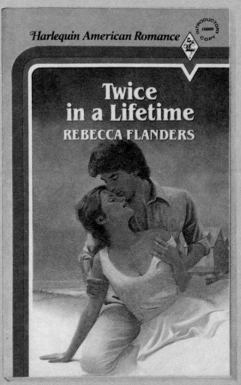

Harlequin American Romance

INTRODUCTORY COPY 16000

Twice in a Lifetime
REBECCA FLANDERS

YOURS FREE!

Enter a uniquely American world of romance with *Harlequin American Romance.*™

Harlequin American Romances are the first romances to explore today's new love relationships. These compelling romance novels reach into the hearts and minds of women across America...probing into the most intimate moments of romance, love and desire.

You'll follow romantic heroines and irresistible men as they boldy face confusing choices. Career first, love later? Love without marriage? Long-distance relationships? All the experiences that make love real are captured in the tender, loving pages of *Harlequin American Romance*.

What makes American women so different when it comes to love? Find out with *Harlequin American Romance!* Send for your introductory FREE book now.

GET THIS BOOK FREE!

MAIL TO:
Harlequin Reader Service
649 Ontario Street
Stratford, Ontario N5A 6W2

YES! I want to discover *Harlequin American Romance*.
Send me FREE and without obligation, "Twice in a Lifetime."
If you do not hear from me after I have examined my FREE
book, please send me the 4 new *Harlequin American Romance*
novels each month as soon as they come off the presses. I
understand that I will be billed only $2.25 per book (total
$9.00). There are no shipping or handling charges. There
is no minimum number of books that I have to purchase.
In fact, I may cancel this arrangement at any time. "Twice
in a Lifetime" is mine to keep as a FREE gift, even if I do
not buy any additional books.   354-CIA-2ABZ

Name   (please print)

Address   Apt. No.

City   State/Prov.   Zip/Postal Code

Signature (If under 18, parent or guardian must sign.)

This offer is limited to one order per household and not valid to current
Harlequin American Romance subscribers. We reserve the right to
exercise discretion in granting membership. If price changes are
necessary, you will be notified. Offer expires March 31, 1984.

PRINTED IN U.S.A.

Experience *Harlequin American Romance*™...

with this special introductory FREE book offer.

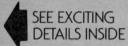 **SEE EXCITING DETAILS INSIDE**

Send no money. Mail this card and receive this new, full-length *Harlequin American Romance* novel absolutely FREE.

Business Reply Mail

No Postage Stamp Necessary if Mailed in Canada

Postage will be paid by

Harlequin Reader Service

649 Ontario Street

Stratford, Ontario

N5A 9Z9

but had a little cottage just outside it. As the old lady took them into her living-room Julie looked about her in amazement. She hadn't realised places like this really existed—the old-fashioned furniture, the faded photographs on the wall; a small fire was burning in the grate despite the season, the old lady was wearing a Paisley pinafore over her tweed skirt and pink twin-set.

And lying in front of the fire, looking very comfortable, was presumably the subject of their story. Sammy was a huge ginger tabby, opening baleful eyes to glare at them for disturbing his sleep.

Mrs Tibbles proved to be a twittering little woman, full of the fact that her darling Sammy had been saved from the jaws of death by his woeful miaowing. After receiving a vicious scratch from him Julie was inclined to think that Sammy shouldn't have been so darned nosy in the first place.

'That's my husband, Harry.' Mrs Tibbles had caught her looking at a very old faded photograph of a very handsome man in his early twenties.

'He's very good-looking.' Julie turned with a smile; Sharon was outside trying to catch up with Sammy, who had decided he had been the focus of enough attention lately, and had run out of the house.

Mrs Tibbles picked up the photograph, her lined face softened with love. 'He was until the day he died.'

'Oh, I'm sorry!' Julie was instantly contrite. 'I didn't realise.'

'Don't be sorry, my dear.' Mrs Tibbles put the photograph back on the sideboard and turned to pour the tea she had insisted on giving them. 'If I didn't think we were going to be together again one day maybe I'd be sad too. But we loved each other so much I have no doubts.'

'Do you have any children?' Julie accepted the cup of tea.

'My only regret is that I decided not to have any,' the elderly woman said softly. 'Harry and I always seemed so complete without them. Now I wish that I hadn't made that decision.'

'But your marriage must have been good. Maybe if you'd had children it wouldn't have been.'

'Harry would have made a good father,' Mrs Tibbles said sadly. 'I just wasn't sure I would make a good mother. Now I think I would have been. Are you married, my dear?'

'I—No.' Julie was conscious of Sharon perhaps coming back at any moment, although she blushed at the lie.

'Career-woman?'

'Er—yes,' she admitted reluctantly.

Mrs Tibbles smiled. 'I keep up with the times. But a career can't keep you warm in bed at night.'

Julie blushed. 'No.'

'I hope I'm not talking out of turn, my dear, but a career can't last you a lifetime either. And there's nothing more fulfilling than having your husband come home to you at night.'

'What if he doesn't?' Julie asked.

'He will if he knows you love him. I loved my Harry very much, and in an effort to hang on to that magical first love I decided I wouldn't have children, that I would keep romance alive.'

'Yes?' Julie had stiffened now.

'But love changes anyway. It has to. You certainly couldn't live the whole of your life in that state of heady excitement,' the old lady teased.

'I suppose not.'

'Of course you couldn't,' the old lady said briskly.

'But when I said love changes I didn't mean it lessened. It grows, becomes deeper, becomes such a part of you that you feel together even when you're apart.'

Julie bit her lip. 'Why are you telling me all this, Mrs Tibbles?'

The old lady shook her head, her eyes sad. 'Because in a way you remind me of me when I was young. Oh, women have a lot more freedom nowadays than I ever had,' she smiled. 'But nevertheless, there's something about you . . . I just wanted you to know that even though I had my Harry I still feel I missed out on a lot of things.'

'As you said, things weren't so liberated for women in those days——'

'No, I don't mean those sort of things,' the other woman dismissed. 'I mean that through my selfishness, my fear of sharing Harry with children, I denied us both a lot of things. I wouldn't have meant any less to him for having his children, for sharing him, in fact I would probably have gained from it. In a lot of marriages children bring you even closer together.'

'And in a lot of them they drive you apart,' Julie said bitterly.

'As you say,' Mrs Tibbles nodded. 'There are two sides to it. But I wouldn't want you to make the wrong decision like I did.'

'Mrs Tibbles——' Julie broke off as Sharon joined them and the talk became general, and if Julie was a little subdued no one mentioned it.

She made the drive back to town automatically. What Mrs Tibbles had said had disturbed her. A woman she had never met before had guessed at the real reason she hadn't wanted children, the reason she had continued working. Maybe Zack had always been too close to the problem to be able to guess the reason for it, but it was somehow unnerving to have a complete stranger guess the truth.

She had been frightened, terrified that Zack would become bored with her, that as Mrs Tibbles had so rightly pointed out, she would become less important to Zack if they had children.

Maybe if she had loved him less, or if he had loved her less, she would have been able to accept the inevitable indifference, the possible breakdown of their marriage when they had two or three children, of Zack leaving her for a younger woman.

As it happened, Teresa was older than her, possibly in her early thirties, but she would be better as a wife for Zack, wouldn't expect so much from him, certainly not total commitment.

Oh, how she still loved him! Her only consolation was that Zack couldn't possibly know that. During the whole night of love they had shared, no words of love had passed either of their lips, indeed they had hardly spoken at all.

When she reached home later that night she knew without doubt that Zack no longer felt anything for her. She received notification of their divorce in the mail.

After that things took a definite downward plunge, and were not helped by a bad bout of 'flu. At first she thought it was a cold, but when she fainted at the office she knew it was time to take to her bed until she felt better.

The only trouble was she didn't feel better, not even when the 'flu had passed, and she felt so tired all the time.

'Pregnancy often makes you feel like that in the first few weeks,' the doctor told her when she visited him.

Pregnancy! Heavens, why hadn't she thought of that?—the tiredness, the occasional feelings of weakness, the nausea at the thought of fried food. She should have realised ... All the signs had been there and she had missed them all. Her night with Zack hadn't been premeditated by either of them, and the idea of pregnancy had been far from either of their minds.

But she had no intention of telling Zack about this baby; she intended asking him for nothing.

'I've lost weight.' She looked worriedly at the doctor.

'That isn't unusual during the first months.' He smiled. 'Don't worry, you'll put weight on soon enough!'

'Yes,' she gave a rueful smile.

'In the meantime,' he handed her a sheet of paper, 'these are the dos and don'ts. Although there aren't many don'ts any more. This pregnancy is perfectly normal, my dear,' he assured her gently. 'Enjoy it, hmm?'

She tried hard to do that over the next few weeks, and the weight did go back on, in fact with her natural slenderness it wouldn't be long before her pregnancy became obvious. She had no idea what she was going to do then.

'Your 'flu's dragging on, isn't it?' Connie frowned at her worriedly when she came up to London and called in after her shopping.

'A bit.' Julie avoided her friend's eyes.

'Have you seen a doctor?'

'Yes. He says it's just a bug I've picked up.'

'It isn't Zack, is it?'

'Zack?' Julie looked up sharply, dark circles beneath her luminous green eyes; 'morning sickness' was taking its toll with her. 'I don't understand?'

'I meant the divorce . . .'

'I agreed to that, Connie.' She almost sighed her relief that Connie hadn't guessed at her real feelings for Zack. 'I haven't changed my mind.'

'Sure?'

'Very sure,' she said firmly.

'We haven't seen much of Zack lately.'

'Is that unusual?'

'I don't know,' Connie frowned. 'He seems—well, different.'

Julie drew in a deep breath. 'Connie, I realise you're concerned, and that Zack is your brother-in-law, but his welfare is no longer of any interest to me.'

'I can't believe that——'

'Believe it, Connie,' she insisted hardly. 'Zack is no longer a part of my life.'

'And Steve?'

'That's finished too,' she revealed reluctantly.

'I liked him.'

'So did I.'

'Then why——'

'Because I only liked him. Stop matchmaking, Connie,' Julie chided impatiently.

'Zack didn't have anything to do with it, did he?'

Julie grimaced. 'What do you think?'

'I think he did,' her friend nodded. 'He was out to cause trouble that weekend.'

'Maybe.'

'And you're angry with him?'

'No,' Julie sighed.

'But you are. I can tell, you're different towards him.' She stiffened. 'I don't know what you mean.'

Connie nodded. 'Before you were indifferent towards him, cold almost. Now you simply avoid talking about him or get angry.'

Julie stood up in her agitation, the straightness of her skirt already showing the beginning of a thickening waistline. 'Maybe I'm just tired of talking about him.

You've become rather obsessed with him lately,' she softened her voice to take the sharpness out of her words.

'I'm worried about him,' Connie confessed.

'Then talk to Ben, not me!'

'You're his wife——'

'Teresa is the one you should be talking to,' Julie said vehemently. 'Teresa, his future wife, not me.'

Connie chewed her bottom lip. 'Ben says they've argued.'

Julie shrugged to hide how this news affected her. 'Maybe she's chafing at how long the divorce is taking. It does seem rather slow.' She had heard nothing more since giving her lawyer the notification of divorce.

'Ben says they've argued badly.'

'I'm not interested,' Julie said through stiff lips. 'If I never see or hear anything about Zack again it will be too soon!'

Unfortunately life can't be that kind. Just when you think you're getting your life back together it deals you another blow.

Doug called her into his office late Monday afternoon. 'Press conference,' he told her abruptly.

She was already putting her jacket on. 'Where?'

'The *Global News*.'

'The *Global News* . . .?' Julie repeated dazedly, all colour leaving her face.

'Zachary Reedman's just taken over a magazine in Italy. He's going to give all the details in——' he looked at his wrist-watch. 'Twenty minutes.'

She swallowed hard, fighting down the nausea. 'Why doesn't he keep it as an exclusive?'

Doug shrugged. 'Publicity, I expect. This is his first step into Europe.'

'Who knows, the world next?' she joked lamely.

'Maybe,' Doug nodded. 'Make sure you ask him that.'

'I——' she licked suddenly dry lips. 'Do I have to do this one, Doug? I—I'd rather you gave it to someone else.'

'It's yours, Julie,' he told her firmly.

'I'd rather not.'

'I'm not asking, Julie, I'm telling,' he said in a voice that brooked no argument.

She could tell that unless she actually collapsed at his feet this was one argument she was going to lose. Besides, if what Steve had said about everyone knowing she had had an affair with Zack was true, then Doug probably already knew the reason she didn't want to do this story. She was just increasing his speculation.

'Is Matt coming with me?' The other man had completely recovered from the gunshot-wound and had been back at work a couple of weeks now.

'Steve's with you this time. He——'

'I'm here,' he said from behind them, his camera already in his hand. 'Ready, Julie?'

She looked at him pleadingly, although she knew there was no way he could help her out of this. The sympathy in his eyes seemed to say he would help her all he could.

'Ready,' she said in a strong voice. 'Let's go.'

It didn't take long to reach the *Global News*; all the major dailies were in Fleet Street. Julie was still shaking as they went up to the boardroom on the eighth floor.

'All right?' Steve prompted huskily.

Far from it, but she wasn't going to turn tail and run now. 'I'm a reporter, aren't I?' she said brightly.

'And reporters don't have emotions?'

'So it's reputed.'

'Then it's reputed wrong.' He took hold of her arm.

'You look as if you're about to pass out.'

Julie felt it too. 'I'll be fine,' she assured him. 'Just don't let go of me, hmm?'

'It's a deal!' he grinned.

Zack sat at the head of the long table, a man either side of him, although they both paled into insignificance next to Zack, the dark pin-striped suit and snowy white shirt giving him an air of distinction, the grey hair at his temples adding to that impression.

He looked in their direction as she and Steve moved quietly into the already full room. Representatives from all the other major newspapers were already here. His eyes were cold as his gaze swept over her, no sign of recognition there.

Colour slowly tinged her cheeks, her huge green eyes dominating her face as the colour ebbed again. She hadn't seen Zack since she had fallen asleep in his arms, and her embarrassment was acute.

But she needn't have worried, his gaze moved on again without even a flicker of emotion on his hard face. Her legs felt shaky as he began to talk, outlining the magazine he had taken over in Italy, the fact that it was a magazine that dealt with fashion, concentrating mainly on the female population. Once he had given them the briefest outline of his future plans for the magazine he invited questions.

The questions were endless, and Zack answered them all calmly and precisely, never once consulting the notes in front of him or the men at his side. Steve moved forward to take photographs, dragging Julie along with him.

She was only feet away from Zack now, so close to the man that she loved, and who was the father of her baby.

'Does the acquisition of this magazine mean you'll be

spending more time out of England?' The question was
asked with cool clarity—and with a feeling of horror
she recognised her own voice!

Cool grey eyes narrowed on her. 'Do you imagine
I'm leaving England, Miss Slater?' Zack's tone was no
longer friendly but mocking now as he answered her.

She tightly clutched her notebook in front of her. 'I
merely—wondered.'

'Then don't. I have no intention of leaving England.'

'Er—but does this mean you'll be spending more time
out of the country?' she persisted.

His eyes cooled even more, his mouth hardening.
'Again no, Miss Slater. I am not handling the running
of this magazine myself. I'm sorry to disappoint you.'

'Oh, you haven't—I mean, why should I care if you
leave England?' She blushed at how rude that sounded,
receiving several curious looks.

'Why indeed?' he drawled.

Her head went back. 'I hear you have plans to marry,
Mr Reedman,' she said curtly. 'Will this interfere with
those plans at all?'

'I fail to see what the purchase of a magazine has to
do with my private life,' he returned icily.

To Julie it was as if they were the only two people in
the room, everyone else here ceasing to exist. 'I'm sure
the public would like to know,' she challenged.

'The public, Miss Slater?' he taunted.

'Yes.' She flushed.

He gave an impatient sigh. 'The purchase of the
magazine does not change any of my own personal
plans,' he told her coldly. 'Now if Miss Slater has
finished this line of questioning perhaps someone else
has some more—relevant questions to ask.'

It was a cruel put-down and Julie paled as the room
seemed to sway, her surroundings beginning to blur.

'For heaven's sake, someone catch her!' Zack was on his feet, not quickly enough to stop her falling himself as he moved hurriedly around the table.

She swayed into Steve's arms, at once feeling safe—she had been sure she was going to crash to the floor and hurt the baby. And she couldn't have suffered that . . .

'Julie!' Zack was at her side, the aloofness gone as he made no effort to hide his concern.

'I—I'm fine.' She was recovering fast, the colour slowly coming back into her cheeks. 'It's the room, it's so warm in here, there's no air.'

He frowned down at her, feeling her fevered cheek. 'It's air-conditioned, quite cool in fact.'

'She hasn't been well——'

'When I want your advice I'll ask for it,' Zack cuttingly interrupted Steve. 'Is it true, Julie?' he lowered his voice, his searching gaze on her face. 'Aren't you well?'

'I had 'flu.' She could stand on her own now, avoiding all the curious faces of the people who were wondering what the owner of the *Global News* was doing fussing over the near-faint of a *Daily Probe* reporter, and calling her 'Julie' instead of the more formal 'Miss Slater' of a moment ago.

'Connie mentioned it,' he still frowned. 'But that was weeks ago.'

She shrugged. 'It's lingering on.'

'You look ill——'

'I'm fine. And have you forgotten we have an audience?' she warned softly, conscious of his hand still caressing her cheek.

His eyes flashed angrily. 'Damn the lot of them! I want to talk to you——'

'Not here, Zack,' she agonised, moving away from

him. 'If you'll excuse me, Mr Reedman,' she said loudly for their listening audience, 'I'll go home and rest. I'm sorry to have interrupted you.'

'Julie——'

'Steve?' she prompted, ignoring Zack as Steve accompanied her out of the room, her head high as she heard the buzz of conversation suddenly start behind her.

Steve grabbed her arm once they were outside, stopping her progress. 'Are you really all right?' he frowned. 'You look terrible.'

'What a boost to my ego you are!' she taunted, pressing the button for the lift. 'Do you think I have enough for a story?' She chewed on her lip. 'Doug is going to love me!'

'Don't you ever think of anything but work?' Steve growled as they went down to the ground floor. 'You just fainted——'

'Almost fainted,' she corrected coolly. 'I told you, it was hot in there.'

'It was normal——'

Julie shrugged. 'It didn't seem it to me. Let's get back to the office, I have to get this story written up.'

'Julie——'

'Please, Steve, just leave it.'

'It was rough on you, wasn't it?' he asked shrewdly.

'What was?'

'Meeting Reedman like that. Doug doesn't know just what a star reporter he has,' he derided.

Julie didn't bother to answer him. She and Steve had worked together several times during the last few weeks, and for the main part it had gone well. It was only occasionally, like now, that he allowed his bitterness to interfere with their working relationship.

It was late when she finally left the paper. Most of

the staff who had come on with her this morning had left for the day long ago, but then most of them had someone or something to go home to. She had never been so conscious of her lack of family, of emotional ties, as she had been lately.

The flat seemed as unwelcoming as usual, the liver she had put out for her dinner even more so. She ate the latter with a green salad, mainly because she knew the doctor would be annoyed with her if she wasn't fit and well the next time she visited him. He was taking every care of her and the baby.

She deliberately kept thoughts of Zack at bay, wouldn't allow herself to dwell on the meeting with him earlier. Although meetings like that hadn't occurred during the last three years she had always been conscious that they could, and it was only good luck that had meant they hadn't. But she was aware that with them both being in the newspaper world the chance happenings could happen again.

What was going to happen when the baby was born she daren't even think. Other single parents managed, so why shouldn't she? She wasn't exactly poor. She would survive somehow, and without Zack's help.

When the doorbell rang and interrupted her worrying she could only feel relief, although when she saw it was Zack that relief turned to apprehension.

'What do you want?' She was instantly hostile.

He was still wearing the pin-striped suit, still looked as dark and distinguished. 'Where the hell have you been?' he attacked. 'I've been calling you all evening!'

Her eyes widened. 'I've been home at least half an hour.'

'And I've been travelling here that amount of time.' He scowled. 'For all I knew you could have been a crumpled heap on the floor.'

'Injured and unable to call for help?' she scorned, to hide her nervousness. She looked a mess, her hair needed combing, her skirt and blouse were crumpled from a day's wear, and she was very conscious of her untidiness in the face of Zack's impeccable appearance.

'You could have been,' he snapped, his eyes narrowed to grey slits. 'After your behaviour earlier I wasn't sure how you were.'

'I've been working, your story—remember?'

He shook his head in disgust. 'You never stop, do you?'

'Never,' she agreed fiercely.

'And are you all right now?' His gaze searched her face. 'You still look pale.'

'Concern, Zack?' she mocked.

'Of course I'm concerned——'

'I don't see why. You haven't given a thought about me the last three years, so why worry now when I feel a little faint?'

'You still feel ill?' he pounced.

'Oh, for Pete's sake!' she gave an angry sigh. 'We women have these little—complexities, you know.'

'I see,' he nodded his head. 'But that's all it is?'

'Yes.'

His mouth twisted derisively, his eyes mocking. 'Can I come in, or do I have to stand on the doorstep all evening?'

Her grip on the door tightened. 'Haven't we spoken enough already? You've satisfied yourself that I'm not prostrate on the floor, don't you have somewhere else to go now?'

'Nowhere that I would rather be.' He gently pushed the door open and went through to the lounge. 'This really is a nice flat,' he looked about him appreciatively.

'I didn't have the chance to look around last time I was here.'

'You were too busy throwing out accusations.' Julie had followed him, watching as he slowly walked around the room.

'Yes, I was, wasn't I?' Zack suddenly looked at her. 'And then Carter arrived. Is he coming here tonight?'

'I—No, not tonight.'

'Then you—oh darn!' he swore as he kicked into her handbag as it lay next to the armchair, going down on his haunches to pick up the things that had fallen out on to the carpet. 'You always did have a habit of leaving these stupid things lying about,' he muttered.

Julie bent down to help him. 'And you always had a habit of kicking them.' She snatched up a container of pills before he did, pushing them to the bottom of the bag.

'Sleeping pills?' he asked sharply.

'No,' she answered truthfully, the iron pills the doctor had given her to take during her pregnancy now safely buried at the bottom of her bag. 'Just something the doctor gave me after my 'flu.'

Zack seemed to accept that they were vitamins or something like that, and got to his feet to pace the room moodily, his hands thrust into his trouser pockets.

Julie watched him, seeing the different emotions flickering across his face. 'Look, Zack,' she sighed, 'I think you should go. I really am feeling fine now. And I must say your concern comes as something of a surprise after—well, after—I haven't heard from you for weeks.'

'Since we spent the night together,' he held her gaze steadily. 'That's what I want to talk to you about.'

'Oh yes?' Once again she was wary.

'Yes,' he sighed. 'I can't stand it any more, Julie. I'm going quietly insane. I want you, and I have to have you.' He looked at her with tortured eyes, a pulse beating erratically in his hard cheek. 'Can you understand that?'

Yes, she could understand that. And hope began to fill her heart as she saw the naked desire in his eyes. Maybe there was hope for them after all, maybe if she could talk to him, explain about the past, tell him about——

He drew in a ragged breath. 'So I've come here tonight willing to offer you what you always wanted.'

Julie frowned. 'What I—always wanted?' she voiced uncertainly.

'Yes,' he hissed. 'You always wanted an affair. Our one night together showed me one thing, Julie—we're still explosive in bed together. So, you always wanted an affair—well, now I do too. I want an affair with you, Julie.'

CHAPTER SEVEN

'I—*What* did you say?' Julie choked disbelievingly.

'I want you, Julie. I want an affair with you.'

She searched his granite-like features, the hard grey eyes, the flaring nostrils and set compressed mouth, the firm thrust of his jaw, the very stance of his body, and knew that he meant this horror. Zack really meant it, he wanted an affair with her!

'No!' she rasped.

'No?' he choked.

'You heard me,' she flashed. 'Just what do you think I am——'

'I know what you are, Julie,' he groaned. 'You're beautiful, desirable, and I badly need to make love to you again. I fought it—oh, how I fought it!' His hands clenched and unclenched at his sides. 'After our anniversary, after I saw you again, I began to want you. I tried to put you from my mind, but no matter what I did, where I went, who I was with, I was always imagining it was you.'

'Teresa——'

'Guessed,' he sighed. 'And when I cried out your name instead of hers one night ...! She quite rightly told me to get out until I have you out of my system.'

'I'm sorry if you feel I've ruined things between you and Teresa,' Julie told him stiffly. 'But that's no reason to come here and insult me.'

'Insult you?' he repeated harshly. 'Admitting how badly I want to make love to you is insulting you?'

'Yes!' she glared at him. 'I'm a person, not some *commodity* you can buy simply because you want it!'

'Buy?' he repeated softly. 'What price do you put on yourself, Julie?'

A red haze passed in front of her eyes, not of weakness this time but of burning anger. 'I don't have a price,' she snapped. 'Have you forgotten that you've already had me, free, gratis, for nothing?'

Zack was grey beneath his tan. 'It was that single night with you that showed me I have a long way to go to get you out of my system. I thought that one night would be enough, that the hunger that had been eating me up for days would finally go away. Instead it's increased, made it impossible for me to think of anything else.'

'And you've decided an affair is the answer to this hunger,' she said dully.

'Yes,' he rasped harshly.

'And just how long would you expect the—affair to last? A week, a month, a year?' Her voice cracked with anger.

'As long as it takes!' he snapped. 'How the blazes do I know?'

'And what do I get out of it?'

'Me.'

Her eyes widened incredulously. 'You?'

'Yes, me,' his mouth twisted. 'You can't have forgotten that you enjoyed that night together as much as I did.'

Colour blazed in her cheeks. 'I should have known you would throw that in my face——'

'I'm not throwing it in your face,' Zack sighed, running a weary hand over his eyes. 'We were always good together physically. I don't think either of us would ever deny that.'

'Maybe not. But I've tried living with you, Zack, and I don't like it.'

'You wouldn't be living with me. We would continue to live separately.'

'And you would just pop over here every time you feel like making love to me,' she derided.

'No,' he flushed. 'Because if I did that I *would* be living here. We could meet whenever it's mutually convenient.'

'Whenever you can get away from Teresa?'

'Teresa?' he frowned. 'I already told you——'

'Surely now that you've decided an affair with me is the answer you can go ahead with your plans to marry Teresa?' she scorned.

'I don't think that would be a very good idea,' he said distantly. 'For Pete's sake, Julie, stop making this difficult for me!'

'For you?' she exclaimed disbelievingly. 'You come here under the pretence of enquiring after my health, and end up offering me an affair, and I'm supposed to make things *easy* for you!'

Zack looked angry too now. 'I'm sure you didn't have this difficulty in arranging your affairs with Clarke and Carter.'

'I didn't have an affair with Alec!' Her voice was shrill. 'That one time you found me in his arms I was crying because I'd had an argument with you. Maybe I should have had an affair with him, maybe then I wouldn't have given a darn about your accusations. At least they would have been true!'

'And Carter?'

She stiffened. 'I don't intend telling you anything about Steve and myself. Alec you have a right to an explanation about—although heaven knows I've made it often enough! Steve came after our separation, so he's none of your business. I will say this, though, there was never any affair arranged between us. In case you didn't know it, those sort of things are supposed to happen spontaneously.'

'And did they happen—spontaneously, often?'

'As often as we both wanted them to!'

'What's so different about my proposal?'

The fact that it wasn't a proposal! Having been Zack's wife she couldn't accept anything less from him. 'The answer is no, Zack,' she told him woodenly.

'Why?' He pulled her round to face him. 'You enjoyed the night we spent together two months ago as much as I did.'

'That doesn't mean I want to repeat it,' she snapped.

'Don't you? Don't you really?' he said softly, pulling her closer and closer to him. 'I think I can prove to you that you do.'

'No!' she began to struggle. 'Zack, no!'

'Julie, I have to. Believe me, I can't stop myself,' he murmured against her throat. 'If I could, I would. You're driving me insane,' his hands ran feveredly over her body. 'I remember, I remember—God, how I remember!'

She pushed away from him as his lips would have claimed hers. 'And I remember what it was like being with you last time—the jealousy, the suspicion, the oppression——'

'It wouldn't be like that this time. We wouldn't make any claims on each other——'

'We won't, because there isn't going to be an affair.' She turned away from him, her hands shaking with reaction. 'I want you to leave, Zack. And I don't want you to come back.'

He gave a ragged sigh. 'I can't stay away.'

'Then I won't let you in.'

'I could camp out on your doorstep.'

'Then I'll go away,' she said desperately.

'No!' his voice was sharp. 'Don't do that, Julie. Maybe we could have dinner one evening——'

She shook her head. 'That wouldn't be a good idea.'

'We could talk——'

'And after we'd talked you would expect to be asked to share my bed!'

A pulse beat erratically at his jaw. 'Don't despise me for wanting you, Julie,' he rasped.

'I don't,' she sighed. 'I just—Even an affair with you is too much.'

'You hate me that much?' He paled.

'I don't think it was ever hate, Zack. I've been angry, hurt, but I don't think there was ever real hate there.'

'Then I won't give up,' he decided firmly. 'You should know by now, Julie, I can be very determined.'

'Yes,' she acknowledged ruefully.

'Then expect to see a lot of me in future,' he warned on his way out.

Expect to see a lot of him! How could she do that when she was expecting his baby? Another month and it would really begin to show on her slender frame. She would have to get away before that happened.

Zack kept his word not to give up, seeming to know her actions before Julie knew them herself, often picking her up from work if she happened to work late. At first she had refused, claiming the quite valid excuse of having her own car with her, but then her MG had to go in for servicing, and for several days she was left without a car. Zack seemed to know as if by magic, and turned up at her flat that first morning, taking her to and from work the whole of the week her car was off the road.

He appeared at Connie and Ben's when she went down for a visit too, even turned up at her flat one Saturday afternoon to take her shopping.

'I remember you like to shop on a Saturday afternoon.' He turned to smile at her, having made her an unwilling passenger in his car once again.

'You really will have to stop this, Zack,' she sighed. 'I see more of you now than I did when we were married,' she added ruefully.

'Considering I only saw you fifty-six days out of our year of marriage that wouldn't be too difficult,' he told her in a steely voice.

'Fifty-six . . .? I don't believe that!' she gasped.

'I counted them, Julie,' he said bleakly. 'I can even give you dates if you want them.'

'That won't be necessary,' she refused abruptly.

Fifty-six days out of a whole year? Could Zack possibly be right? She had a dreadful feeling he was. She had travelled a lot in those days, had always accepted any job that took her abroad, believing the separations strengthened, not weakened, their marriage. Their almost second-honeymoons when she returned home had seemed to confirm this.

'You should have stopped me if you didn't like it,' she told him now.

He gave her a mocking glance. 'And be accused of blocking your career? No, my dear Julie, I couldn't do that. If it had bothered you then you would have put a stop to it yourself, but it obviously didn't.'

'It wasn't that——' she broke off, flushing.

'No?'

'Er—no.' She had said too much, had aroused his curiosity now.

'Then what was it?'

She picked up her handbag. 'Could you drop me off

here?' she requested brightly. 'I want to go into this antique shop and choose something for Connie and Ben's wedding anniversary.'

'Lord, that's next week, isn't it,' Zack groaned. 'Thanks for reminding me. If I park the car I can come with you——'

'Some other time. Thanks for the lift, Zack,' she added pointedly.

With a frustrated sigh in her direction he pulled over to the side of the road, barely giving her time to get out on to the pavement before accelerating away under pressure from the traffic building up behind him.

Beside the fact that Julie tried to have as little as possible to do with Zack there was a second reason she didn't want him about today. All her clothes were becoming uncomfortable about the waist, the tailored ...ts she wore to work particularly so, and today she had decided to buy herself more suitable clothing for a pregnant lady. The last thing she needed was Zack at her side.

Nevertheless she kept giving hounded looks over her shoulder, as if expecting Zack to join her, even though she had lost no time in choosing a gift for Connie and Ben and going on to the other shops, disappearing into the crowd of Saturday shoppers.

She didn't choose blatantly maternity dresses, more something in between, nothing that clung or was shaped to her waist but not looking like a bell-tent either. There would be plenty of time for the latter in a few more months!

Zack didn't put in an appearance, and it was with some relief that Julie made her way back to her flat, with a beautiful glass lamp for Connie and Ben, and ...lf a dozen new dresses to hide her condition.

Zack was leaning against the wall outside her flat,

and came forward to take the parcels out of her hand. 'I'm glad I decided to wait here,' he drawled mockingly.

Julie unlocked her door, going inside to dispose of all the parcels in her bedroom. 'I suppose it wouldn't do any good to ask you to leave?' she said resignedly.

He had already settled himself in one of the armchairs, casually dressed in dark blue trousers and a light blue sweater, his hair very dark against the latter. 'None at all,' he confirmed lightly.

'I—A cup of tea?' she offered nervously.

'I'll get it.' He rose agilely to his feet. 'You look tired.'

Probably because she was! 'You don't know where anything is——'

'Then I'll find it.' He gently pushed her down into an armchair and bent to take off her shoes. 'Put your feet up.' He placed the stool in front of her.

She did so, leaning back with her eyes closed as Zack went into the kitchen to make the tea. It was a luxury to have someone wait on her in this way, and she took full advantage of it.

'You look better already.' Zack came back with a tray of tea, having managed, with his usual efficiency, to find all the necessary equipment. He put the tray down in front of her. 'You can be mother,' he grinned as she picked up the teapot.

It instantly slipped out of her hand, hitting the side of the coffee-table and spilling the boiling liquid all over her and the carpet.

'Julie!' Zack grabbed hold of her hand, pulling her into the kitchen to quickly wipe the hot tea from her legs, his expression one of anxiety. 'Does it hurt?'

'No.' She couldn't feel the pain. 'You can be mother,' he had said. Lord, he didn't know how true that was going to be in a few months' time!

Just at that moment the telephone began ringing. 'I'll get it,' Zack told her. 'You finish cleaning yourself up,' he instructed gravely.

'The carpet——'

'Can wait a while.' He strode off to answer the telephone, back within seconds. 'It's Connie,' he informed her, looking her over critically. 'Are you all right?' he queried softly.

Julie put the towel down. 'Yes. Connie, you said,' she asked agitatedly.

'Mm,' he grimaced. 'I'm afraid I've aroused her curiosity by answering the call.'

She had been afraid of that. 'The carpet——'

'For Pete's sake stop fussing about the carpet!' he snapped. 'Did you burn yourself?' He looked down at the slender length of her legs.

'Only a little.'

'Where?' He was instantly alert.

Her cheeks flushed bright red. 'Just on the ankle. I'd better go and talk to Connie.'

Zack scowled. 'All right,' he allowed. 'But don't be long. You need to put some cream on those burns.'

'Zack——'

'Connie,' he reminded her dryly. 'By this time she's probably bursting with curiosity.'

She was—the questions came thick and fast. 'Yes, that was Zack,' Julie sighed confirmation. 'He just called round. No, Connie,' she said firmly, blushing at Zack's taunting look. 'Next Saturday?' she frowned.

'You haven't forgotten Ben and I have an anniversary then?' Connie was scandalised.

'Of course I haven't forgotten.' Julie turned her back on Zack as he began to mop up the tea from the carpet. 'What time do you want me to be there?'

'Seven will be fine.'

She frowned. 'Are you sure you and Ben wouldn't rather celebrate on your own?'

'Not if you and Zack will join us,' Connie said mischievously.

'Zack?' she repeated in a startled voice. 'Oh, but I——'

'Tell her I'd love to come,' he said from behind her in a stage whisper.

She turned to glare at him. 'Did you hear that?' she asked Connie with a sigh.

'Yes,' her friend said excitedly. 'Wait until I tell Ben you're back with Zack!'

'I am not back with Zack!' she retaliated in a fierce voice.

'Seeing him then,' Connie corrected. 'Even that's an improvement. I'll see you both next weekend.'

'Yes,' Julie sighed, and rang off to glare at Zack. 'She has totally the wrong impression,' she told him angrily.

'Never mind,' he dismissed easily. 'Let me have a look at your legs.'

Dark colour flooded her cheeks. 'Leave my legs alone!' She backed away from him.

'Julie!' he frowned.

'They—they're fine,' she insisted. 'It doesn't even sting.'

'Nevertheless——'

'Are you really going next weekend?' she determinedly interrupted him.

'I was invited,' he shrugged.

'And so you're going?'

His eyes narrowed. 'Yes, I'm going. Which means you aren't, hmm?' he asked shrewdly.

'I have to go,' she sighed. 'I told Connie I would.'

'I'll drive you——'

'I'd rather you didn't.'

'Well, I'm going to,' he told her firmly. 'Don't worry, Julie, it's only one night,' he added harshly. 'Just one evening you'll have to spend in my company.'

Oh dear, how ungrateful she was being! Zack had driven her to the shops, made her a cup of tea, fussed over her when she burnt herself, had even cleaned up the mess, and now she was begrudging him a visit to his own brother. And the lift would be appreciated if she would stop being so stubborn; the thought of the long drive when she felt so tired all the time was not really a pleasant one.

'What time will you pick me up?' she asked briskly.

Zack looked startled. 'You want me to drive you there after all?'

'If you wouldn't mind,' she nodded.

'I don't mind at all.' He looked pleased with himself. 'Five-thirty, okay?'

She nodded again. 'I'll make another cup of tea,' she suggested as a way of escaping the warmth of his grey eyes.

He frowned. 'You still look pale.'

'I'm fine,' she avoided his eyes.

'Have dinner with me,' he said suddenly, his hands clasping hers, his expression intent.

Julie bit her lip. Another couple of weeks and she was going to be leaving London for good, would probably never see Zack again. She only had another week to work at the *Daily Probe*, having handed in her notice several weeks ago, much to Doug's surprise. He had tried to talk her out of it, but she had remained adamant. She didn't really have any choice!

Could she give herself this one evening with Zack, a time just for the two of them? She felt she could.

'I'd like to,' she accepted almost shyly.

'You would?' His eyes widened in surprise.

'Yes, please.'

'Then forget the tea, I don't really want any. I'll pick you up at seven-thirty.'

Julie could hear the nervous beat of her heart, but she couldn't back out now. One evening of having Zack to herself, that was all she asked. 'Lovely,' she nodded, knowing she would have months, years, for regrets. Tonight was just for the two of them, a final farewell on her part.

She put on one of the new dresses she had bought on her shopping spree, a bottle-green loose-fitting crêpe that darkened the colour of her eyes and highlighted the red of her hair. She felt attractive, and she knew Zack thought the same thing when she opened the door to him later that evening.

'For you.' He held out a single red rose.

Colour flooded her cheeks. On their first date together Zack had bought her a similar red rose. 'Thank you,' she said huskily, tears suddenly shimmering in her eyes.

'Let me,' he offered as she fumbled trying to pin it on her dress, his fingers gentle against the firm swell of her breast, his breathing suddenly ragged as he looked up at her. 'Let's go,' he said in a brisk voice, his hand on her elbow as he escorted her outside.

It was the same restaurant too, a poignant reminder of the many evenings they had spent here when they had been in love and happy together.

'Enjoying yourself?' Zack looked at her with anxious eyes as she sat quietly opposite him.

Julie bit her lip to stop it trembling. 'Why are you doing this? Why this restaurant, Zack?' She looked up at him with hurt green eyes.

He frowned. 'You always used to like it.'

'Yes,' she sighed. 'But first the rose, and now the

restaurant. Why, Zack?' she repeated.

He sat forward to clasp her hand as it rested on the table-top. 'I wanted to bring back the good times, Julie,' he told her huskily. 'Have I ruined things?'

She pulled her hand out of his. 'There's nothing to ruin,' she said distantly.

She had been a fool to come out with him tonight. This evening together meant one thing to her, another to Zack. He had seen it as a sign that she was weakening in her decision not to have an affair with him. He hadn't ruined anything, she had been wanting something that didn't exist.

'Julie——'

'Could we order, please?' she cut across his pleading tone. 'I'm feeling hungry.' And surprisingly she was too; her appetite had never been so good as since she had been pregnant.

Zack drew in a controlling breath, very pale beneath his tan. 'Of course we can order.' He signalled the waiter to their table.

For Julie the evening had been spoilt, and she knew Zack was aware of her disappointment, cutting the evening short to take her home, and insisting on walking her to her door.

He looked down at her for several long minutes, a pulse beating in the hardness of his jaw. 'Julie!' he groaned at last, pulling her into his arms to kiss her with a desperate hunger. 'Oh, Julie, I want you. I need you. Let me come inside with you, darling,' he rested his forehead on hers. 'Let me show you how good it could be between us.'

She moved determinedly out of his arms. 'Do you usually expect to sleep with a woman after one evening together?' She saw him flinch at the coldness of her tone.

A ruddy hue crept into the leanness of his cheeks.

'You're my wife, Julie.'

'I may be,' she accepted stiltedly. 'But that doesn't entitle you to expect to share my bed.'

'Julie——'

'I'll see you on Saturday.' She ignored his pleading look, unlocking the door to her flat. 'Saturday, Zack,' she repeated firmly as she closed the door in his face.

What a fool she had been! You could never bring back the past, could never revive a love that had died . . .

Despite the way they had parted Julie half expected to see Zack during the following week, but there was no sign of him. She didn't know whether to be relieved or upset. Her brain, thinking logically, told her she was relieved, and yet part of her felt disappointed.

But he arrived promptly at five-thirty on Saturday, looking very handsome in a dark dinner suit, his eyes appreciative as he studied her with slow appraisal.

Julie was aware of having that certain bloom about her a lot of pregnant women had; the tiredness and morning sickness had begun to recede now, and her skin had a healthy glow, her hair a deep glossy red. The black dress she was wearing, another one of her new ones, fitted over her bust to fall in soft folds to just below her knees. She looked good, and she was beginning to feel it too.

'Ready?' Zack asked huskily, making no effort to come inside the flat, reminding her all too forcefully that last time she had refused him entrance.

She nodded, letting him take the gaily coloured parcel out of her hands as they went down the stairs.

Zack placed the parcel on the back seat beside his own present for the other couple. 'It's a jade figurine,' he told Julie at her curious look. 'Connie collects them.'

'Yes,' she nodded, feeling awkward with him as she sat primly at his side, leaving London far behind them. He obviously hadn't forgiven her for the other evening. 'Have you had a busy week?' she attempted conversation.

'You sound like a wife!' he taunted.

'Sorry,' she flushed. 'I was only trying to be polite.'

'Were you?' His tone was cold.

'Yes!'

Zack sighed. 'Okay. Yes, I've had a busy week. I've spent most of it in Italy.'

'The magazine?' she asked with interest.

He quirked one dark eyebrow. 'Are you asking as a reporter or as my wife?'

She had stopped being the latter long ago, and she had given up being the former yesterday. 'Neither,' she replied stiltedly. 'Not your mistress either,' she snapped.

'Being polite again, were you?' He appeared unmoved by her show of temper.

'As it happens, yes!'

Zack shrugged. 'There are a few teething troubles with the magazine.'

'That only you could handle.'

'I coped,' he drawled.

'I'm sure you did!' This time her sarcasm was unmistakable.

Zack's mouth tightened angrily. 'You wanted to know, Julie. If you aren't really interested then don't bother to ask.'

'I was interested,' her eyes flashed deeply green. 'You started the sarcasm, don't forget.'

'So I did,' he sighed. 'I'm sorry, Julie. Did you miss me this week?' he quirked one brow.

She shrugged. 'I've been too busy to notice your absence.'

'You're looking better, anyway. Work must agree with you.' He appeared unperturbed by the way she hadn't really answered his question.

'It always did,' she replied tartly. 'Or have you forgotten?'

'No,' he said dryly. 'Are things over between you and Carter now?'

'Steve and I are still friends,' she answered him without actually lying.

'He's a fool,' Zack ground out.

Julie ignored him, and the rest of the journey was made in an uneasy silence. Connie was very pleased with their presents, although she was even more ecstatic over the fact that Julie and Zack had arrived together.

Ben had booked a table at a quiet restaurant not too far away, where the relaxed atmosphere was conducive to conversation. The meal was leisurely, although Julie refused the wine, accepting only a small glass of champagne to toast the happy couple on their fourth wedding anniversary.

'I never knew abstinence was one of your good qualities,' Zack taunted, sitting beside her, opposite the other couple.

She avoided his sharp gaze. 'I had a headache earlier and took two aspirins to clear it,' she invented. 'I wouldn't want to pass out on you again.'

'Headache gone now?' His voice was husky with concern.

'Yes.' She turned to Connie, finding her friend watching them with avid interest. 'Did the children settle down all right tonight?' she changed the subject.

'Fine,' Connie nodded. 'Although Nicholas wanted to stay up when he realised his Aunty Julie and Uncle Zack were coming to dinner.'

Julie didn't like the way that made them sound like a

couple again. One thing she and Zack weren't, and never would be, was back together.

'He was curious to know where his Aunty Teresa was, though,' Ben put in softly.

'Ben!' his wife admonished, and from the wince he gave he also received a painful kick under the table.

He wasn't deterred, looking challengingly at his brother. 'Well, where is she?'

'The last I heard she had gone to America for a holiday,' Zack told him calmly. 'She's been there the last few weeks.'

'And Uncle Steve?' Ben looked mockingly at Julie now.

'At home, I would think,' she flushed. 'Connie didn't include him in the invitation.'

'You aren't going to tell us, are you?' Ben sighed his chagrin.

'Tell you what?' Julie was genuinely puzzled.

'Whether or not the two of you are back together. Connie's been bursting to know all week.'

Julie flushed. 'We——'

'We're thinking about it.' Zack's hand covered hers, his expression warning.

She gave him a resentful look and firmly removed her hand from his. 'Actually, I'm going away for a while,' she dropped her bombshell.

Zack instantly stiffened, his eyes narrowing. 'For a holiday, you mean?'

'No,' she replied calmly. 'I feel like a change of environment, so I'm leaving London for a while.'

'Why?'

She blinked. 'I just told you——'

'And your job?' he rasped. 'Do you feel like getting away from that too?'

'I've already left the *Daily Probe*.'

'The devil you have!' Zack's voice was harsh. 'When did you decide all this?'

She shrugged. 'I've been thinking about it for some time.'

'Like hell you have!' he said tautly. 'You aren't going anywhere, Julie, because I won't let you.'

'You can't stop me!'

'Try me,' he threatened.

'Zack——'

'Stay out of this, Ben,' he turned on his brother. 'Julie is my wife——'

'We're getting a divorce!' she reminded him heatedly.

'We may be,' he agreed grimly, 'but right now we're still married. And you stay put.'

'Zack, you can't——'

'Don't try and run my life, Ben,' he warned, dangerously soft. 'Julie knows very well I have no intention of letting her leave London, not now or in the future.'

'Zack, please,' she looked down at her hands. 'Let's not spoil Connie and Ben's anniversary.'

'You knew I wouldn't accept your leaving London——'

'And I just told you you can't stop me!' her eyes blazed.

'Can't I?'

She flushed at the threat in his voice. The expression in his eyes told her the threat was a physical one, but it certainly wasn't violently so. 'Could we leave?' she said agitatedly. 'We can talk about this some other time, Zack,' she told him firmly.

'I agree,' he nodded grimly. 'We can.'

That time came soon enough, as soon as they got back to her flat. Julie's effort to get out of the car and go inside was foiled by Zack's hold on her arm.

'I'm coming with you,' he said stubbornly.

She held her head high as they went inside the building, unlocking her door with a slightly unsteady hand. Once inside she looked at Zack unflinchingly, determined not to be unnerved by the deep anger in his icy grey eyes.

'Running away isn't going to solve anything,' he said suddenly.

'I'm not running away——'

'What else would you call it?' he rasped. 'You love living in London, you always have—that excuse about needing a change of environment doesn't hold water. You're running away, Julie. From me.'

Her head went back. 'And if I am?'

'I won't let you go!' His fingers bit into her shoulders as he shook her. 'I won't let you go, Julie,' he repeated with a groan. 'You can't tell me that night we spent together meant nothing to you.'

'No,' she acknowledged huskily. How could she, when that single night together had produced a child?

'And that you wouldn't like it to happen again?' he prompted, his face only inches away from her own, his warm breath ruffling her hair.

She closed her eyes to shut out the sight of him, instantly more aware of the smell and feel of him. Her eyes opened in alarm as she felt herself sway towards him.

'It won't happen again, Zack,' she told him firmly.

'Won't it?' His eyes held hers mesmerised as he slowly lowered his head, his mouth taking fierce possession of hers.

She *could* take this last time with him, would make it a present to herself, a time to cherish to her during the lonely years without him.

Her mouth opened invitingly beneath his, her arms

going up about his neck as she pressed herself against him, instantly feeling the hardening of his thighs.

Zack gave a groan as he felt her capitulation, and his mouth instantly softened against hers, coaxing rather than demanding. His hands moved tentatively over her body, almost as if he were afraid he might break the spell of her at last being a willing recipient to his kisses.

His lips moved to caress her throat, one hand cupping her breast through the thin material of her dress, finding the nipple with unnerving accuracy, his touch bringing the nub to full pulsating life.

'I want you, Julie,' he told her throatily.

'Yes.'

'Yes?' He raised his head, his eyes almost black with desire. 'You mean—yes?'

Her laugh caught in her throat. 'That's what yes usually means,' she glowed up at him.

'But——'

Her fingertips over his lips prevented further words. 'No questions, Zack,' she pleaded huskily. 'Just make love to me.'

'Oh, yes!' he moaned. 'Where's your bedroom?'

'This way.' She took his hand to lead the way.

Zack followed as if in a daze, kicking over her handbag on the way. 'Darn!' he looked down irritably at the scattered contents. 'I've done it again.'

'Leave it,' Julie encouraged impatiently.

'Yes. He swore as he stepped on something, a loud crunching noise telling of the damage, and pills fell on to the carpet as he took his foot off the plastic container.

Julie watched in horror as he bent to pick them up, putting the pills on the coffee-table before picking up the crushed container, frowning as he looked at the label.

'Iron,' he muttered. 'But what—You aren't ill, are you?' he frowned.

'No——'

His hand slowly moved out to pick up a white card that had also fallen out of the handbag. He read what was written on it before slowly looking up at Julie. 'What's this?' he asked slowly.

'I—An appointment card,' she answered hollowly, feeling frozen to the spot. If she weren't she would run out of the flat, away from the accusation in Zack's eyes.

He stood up, towering over her ominously. 'Iron pills, and this,' he held up the card.

'It's nothing——'

'Nothing!' he repeated savagely, his face contorted with rage. 'I've seen tablets like this before, Julie. And this,' he held up the appointment card. 'This I can work out for myself. It's an ante-natal card, Julie. And only pregnant women attend ante-natal clinics, as Connie did.'

'I——'

'How pregnant are you?' he demanded to know, his expression cold.

'Very,' she answered almost hysterically, wondering if all this was a bad dream—a very bad dream. Zack wasn't supposed to find out, and he wouldn't have done if she hadn't craved this one last night in his arms.

His eyes glazed, his mouth twisting angrily. 'I meant how many months!' he stormed.

She wet her suddenly dry lips, wondering if she dared lie about this. If Zack thought the child was Steve's he would leave her alone. He would probably never want to come near her again!

'I can always contact the doctor,' he told her with narrowed eyes. 'His name is on this card.'

'He wouldn't tell you——'

'I'm your husband, Julie, he would tell me,' Zack said grimly. 'Well?'

There was no point in lying now—if there ever had been. 'I'm ten weeks pregnant, Zack,' she told him dully. 'Ten weeks.'

'Then the child is mine?'

'You can do your arithmetic as well as I can.'

He grasped her arms, forcing her to look at him. 'Is it mine?' he demanded.

'You know it is!' she flashed rebelliously.

He shook his head, deep lines etched into his face. 'Carter was still in your life ten weeks ago.'

She turned away from him, the curve of her cheek very vulnerable. 'Steve was never my lover,' she mumbled .

'Never?'

'No, never!' She looked up at him resentfully. 'You can please yourself whether or not you believe that. Or ask Steve.'

Zack's mouth twisted. 'I doubt he would be willing to admit to a thing like that.'

'Not all men like to boast about their conquests,' she snapped contemptuously.

'You were never a conquest, Julie, more like a battle well fought,' he rasped. 'So the baby isn't Carter's?'

'You know it's yours, Zack,' she choked, her face buried in her hands. 'Now would you please go?'

'Go?' he repeated harshly. 'I'm not going anywhere.'

Her hands were slowly lowered as she looked at him with shock. 'You have to go. I don't want you here!' she added shrilly, her expression one of panic.

'Too bad,' he taunted. 'That baby is mine, and I'm not letting it out of my sight.'

'You can't stay here,' she gasped.

'What else would you suggest I do?'

'That you go home! You can't stay here,' she repeated desperately, very pale.

'No, maybe I can't,' he agreed slowly. 'Your bedroom is through there, you said.' He strode through to the bedroom, opening her wardrobe and drawers to begin throwing her clothes down on the bed, uncaring of the mess he was making.

Julie watched him for several stunned minutes, suddenly clutching his arm as he pulled the case out of the bottom of the wardrobe. 'What are you doing?' she gasped.

'Packing your clothes,' he said grimly. 'You said I can't stay here—well, now that I know you're having my baby, neither can you.'

'It's my home,' she protested.

'Not any more.' He threw the clothes into the suitcase. 'You're coming to live with me.'

She shook her head, tears not far from the surface. 'I'm going away.'

'No, you aren't. I'm going to make sure you're watched every minute of the day. You aren't going to some private clinic and getting rid of my baby,' he told her coldly.

Her hands dropped to her sides, her face very pale as she slowly took in what he had said. He couldn't really mean that, she must have heard him wrong. 'Getting rid of the baby . . .?' she repeated dazedly.

'I know you, Julie,' he rasped. 'You don't like children, you never wanted them. Heaven knows you told me often enough!'

'And you think I would kill our baby?' she choked.

'I wouldn't be at all surprised,' he said grimly. 'Why else would you leave London?' He closed the case with a snap of the locks. 'Okay, let's go. You can pick up the rest of your things tomorrow.'

'Alone?' she scorned numbly.

'No,' his eyes were cold. 'I'll be with you.'

Julie didn't even attempt to protest any more, too numbed by the thought that Zack actually believed she was capable of killing their baby, was callous enough to rid herself of the baby now growing inside her.

CHAPTER EIGHT

ZACK didn't speak to her on the drive to his home; his expression was grim, his thoughts turning inwards.

Julie didn't talk either. She had no idea what Zack's reaction was to the thought of being a father, she only knew he believed her to be incapable of being a mother. His surprise she would have expected, his anger too, but not this mistrust. The idea of aborting their baby hadn't even occurred to her.

And it didn't now. She wanted this baby, wanted it badly, and no matter what Zack thought, what his plans were, she intended being its mother.

'Zack——'

'Not now, Julie,' he snapped curtly, his jaw rigid. 'I'm likely to get violent.'

'I don't see why——'

'You were going to get rid of my baby!' His hands gripped the steering-wheel so tightly his knuckles showed white. 'I'll never forgive you for that, Julie. Never!'

'I wasn't——'

'You were going away!'

'To have the baby, not get rid of it,' she told him angrily.

'Adopted?' His eyes blazed as he briefly turned to look at her, their colour a light grey in his icy anger.

'Certainly not!' She stiffened. 'This baby is mine, Zack. Not yours, not for adoption, but *mine*. And I intend loving it and keeping it. If you want to be its father then you'd better accept that.'

'I'm *going* to be its father,' he said arrogantly. '*You* had better get used to that idea.'

She licked her lips nervously. 'What does that mean?'

'It means that our marriage will now go on, that there will be no divorce.'

'There may not be any divorce.' She knew that now Zack knew about his child he would never agree to that. 'But the marriage will not go on, not as before anyway,' she said firmly, her tone adamant.

'Meaning?'

'Meaning that I'll live with you, let you take care of the baby, but everything else between us is finished.'

His mouth tightened, a pulse beating erratically in his jaw. 'There will be no other men——'

'No, there won't,' she agreed angrily. 'But not because you said there won't, but because *I* don't want them. You can make your own arrangments.'

His mouth twisted. 'You won't object?'

'As long as you stay away from me I couldn't give a darn what you do!'

And she meant it. The things Zack had said to her, the accusations he had made, were unforgivable. She had forgiven this man so much, this she just couldn't forgive—or forget.

The flat Zack now occupied wasn't the same one they had had when they had lived together last time, although of a similar style, luxuriously so.

A housekeeper came out to greet them, eyeing the suitcase in Zack's hand rather curiously, although obviously she was too well trained to ask questions.

'Miss Barr called from New York, sir,' the housekeeper informed him.

He nodded, his expression still grim. 'Did she leave a message?'

'Just the telephone number where she could be

reached. I left it on your desk, sir.'

'Thank you, Mrs Humphries. Is the blue room made up?'

'Of course, sir,' the woman answered almost indignantly.

'Then show Mrs Reedman where it is,' he instructed curtly. 'And perhaps she'd like some coffee,' he added as an afterthought.

'Mrs Reedman . . .?' the housekeeper repeated dazedly.

'My wife,' he said tersely. 'I'll be in my study if you need me for anything,' and he strode off, a door slamming shut seconds later.

Julie smiled ruefully at the other woman. 'The blue room?' she prompted, deciding that it was up to Zack to make any explanations he felt necessary. If she didn't soon sit down she was going to fall down!

Seconds later she was alone. The blue room was beautifully feminine, a white fluffy carpet on the floor, her feet sinking into it, the quilt on the double bed a deep turquoise, as were the curtains.

Yes, it was a beautiful prison. For that was how she thought of it. She was trapped in a loveless, sterile marriage with a man who despised her. But her baby would have the best of everything, and a father and mother who loved it—even if they couldn't love each other!

Zack was probably talking to Teresa right now, explaining the necessity of taking back his wife. Would Teresa forgive him, tell him that it didn't matter, that she loved him anyway? Somehow Julie didn't think so. There had been a basic honesty about the other woman that she couldn't fail to like. But Zack need never fear a lack of female companionship, there would always be women available to a man of his looks and wealth.

She looked up expectantly as a knock sounded on the door, only it wasn't Mrs Humphries with the coffee who came into the room, it was Zack—a Zack who was a cold, chilling stranger.

He left the door open. 'Is the room to your liking?'

Julie nodded stiffly. 'Thank you.'

'Did you ask Mrs Humphries for some coffee?'

'Yes.'

'Is there anything—any foods,' he added pointedly, 'that upset you?'

She frowned. 'Upset me?'

Zack nodded. 'I remember that Connie couldn't stand anything with tomato in when she was expecting both Nicholas and Suzanne.'

'I see,' she swallowed hard. 'No, I don't have any pet hates yet.'

'Any preferences?'

'Cravings, you mean?'

'Yes.'

He was acting like the head waiter in some expensive hotel! 'I have a definite craving for chocolate,' she told him stiffly. 'Although the doctor told me I shouldn't indulge that craving too often.'

Zack's mouth twisted bitterly. 'It wouldn't do for you to lose your figure, would it?' he taunted.

She looked down at her hands. 'No. What did Miss Barr think of your news? I'm sure she thought, as you no doubt did, that when the time came for you to be a father she would be the mother.'

'Perhaps,' he nodded distantly. 'And she was naturally—upset.'

'I should think that was the least she was! You've treated her very badly, Zack.'

Anger blazed in his icy grey eyes. 'I'm well aware of how I've treated Teresa,' he snapped. 'I don't need your reminder. Her name will not be mentioned between us again.'

'In other words I'm to mind my own business?' Julie mocked.

'Exactly! Ah, Mrs Humphries,' he turned as the housekeeper appeared with the tray of coffee. 'Perhaps you could come to my study for a few moments once you've delivered that? Goodnight, Julie.' His voice instantly chilled.

'Coffee, Mrs Reedman,' the housekeeper smiled at her shyly. 'Would you like breakfast in bed in the morning?' she offered kindly.

The forgotten luxuries of being a rich man's wife started to come back to her. It was years since anyone had offered her breakfast in bed. 'No, I don't think so, thank you,' she refused ruefully. 'I don't want to get into bad habits.'

'Tea, then?'

'Well . . .'

'And a few dry biscuits?' the woman encouraged as she sensed her weakening.

Julie's eyes opened wide with surprise. 'How did you guess, Mrs Humphries?'

The elderly lady smiled. 'I've had three of my own. You have the glow, Mrs Reedman—if you don't mind my saying so.'

She instantly sensed she had a friend in the housekeeper, and returned her smile warmly. 'No, I don't mind at all. And I would prefer coffee and dry toast, if you don't mind.' After a series of trial and error she had discovered this combination helped combat the dreaded morning sickness. 'About seven-thirty, if that's all right?'

'Of course. I——'

'Mrs Humphries?' Zack appeared in the corridor

behind her. 'Are you going to be all night delivering a tray of coffee?' he snapped angrily.

Julie could see the woman's startled surprise at his aggression, and remembering Zack's unfailing politeness in the past to the people who worked for him she thought Mrs Humphries had probably never realised what a foul temper he had when thwarted. The poor woman was almost curtseying by the time she left the room under his eagle-eyed stare.

'I'll see you in the morning,' he told Julie curtly.

She didn't even bother to answer him, but concentrated on pouring her coffee, and the door soon slammed with controlled violence as he left the room.

To her surprise Julie actually slept. She had expected to lie awake all night, and instead slept quite dreamlessly, feeling refreshed and alert by the time Mrs Humphries came in with the coffee and toast the next morning.

'You're looking better today,' she fussed behind Julie, plumping up her pillows.

Julie leant back into the comfort. 'I thought I glowed,' she teased, knowing that whatever Zack had said to Mrs Humphries last night about them, she still had a friend in her.

'You do.' The breakfast table was placed over her legs. 'But yesterday you looked a little tired.'

Julie sipped the coffee, biting lightly on her bottom lip. 'My husband——'

'Should be back soon.'

'Back?' She bit into the toast, feeling the familiar heaving feeling in her stomach.

'He went to your flat to collect some more of your things,' she was told cheerfully.

'But it's only seven-thirty!' Julie gasped.

'Mr Reedman was up at six this morning.'

'Oh.' It seemed that Zack had suffered the insomnia she herself had avoided. And Mrs Humphries didn't seem to have any curiosity about the fact that she wasn't aware of what time Zack had been out of bed, or of the fact that they had separate bedrooms. Maybe Zack had also explained that last night?

She was up and dressed by the time Zack returned, sitting in the lounge, the radio on softly, attempting to read the book on the birth of a baby that she had bought last week. It all sounded rather frightening—beautiful, but frightening all the same.

Zack still looked grim, putting her other two suitcases in her room before coming back to the lounge. 'I closed the lease on your apartment,' he told her arrogantly.

Julie only just managed to bite back her angry retort. After all, she mentally shrugged, she had been moving out anyway. 'Thank you,' she accepted distantly.

If Zack was surprised by her acquiescence he didn't show it. 'I thought you might need these.' He held out her spare bottle of iron tablets to her.

'Thank you,' she said once again as she took them from him.

He gave her an impatient look. 'I think we should talk, Julie.'

She eyed him coolly, ignoring the lines of weariness she could see beside his eyes and mouth. He deserved to be weary. 'About what?'

'This—situation, for one thing.'

'I wouldn't call my pregnancy a situation,' she taunted dryly.

His mouth tightened. 'Don't be difficult, Julie. We can't live the rest of our lives in this state of armed neutrality.'

The rest of their lives! Oh, how ominous that

sounded. She shrugged. 'So we drop our arms.'

'It isn't as easy as that,' Zack scowled down at her.

Julie sighed, her peace once again shattered. 'What do you want now, Zack? What else can I do? I'm here, you're going to have your child, so what else can I do?'

'You can tell me that I was wrong last night, that our child was safe with you.' He looked at her with tortured eyes. 'Can't you tell me that?'

'I already have,' she said woodenly. 'I don't intend begging, Zack. You either believe me or you don't.' Her head was held at a proud angle.

'You couldn't really give a damn?'

Of course she cared, why else did he think she was so hurt by what he had said. 'Not any more,' she shook her head.

'So I believe what I want?'

'Yes.'

'Then I believe you.'

Her brows rose. 'You do?' She couldn't hold back her surprise.

'I have to,' he said gruffly. 'Otherwise we don't stand a chance together.'

'I doubt we do anyway, Zack. Our marriage was at an end once, I think it still is.'

'Maybe,' he acknowledged tersely. 'But we have to try and make something of it. What would you like to do today?'

'Rest,' she shrugged.

His gaze sharpened. 'I realise now this must be the reason you fainted at the press conference, your feelings of weakness. You're all right in yourself, aren't you?'

'Would you care if I weren't?'

'Are you?' he rasped harshly at her cold tone.

'Yes, of course I am,' she snapped. 'A lot of women feel faint, tired. It's nothing unusual.'

'Nevertheless, I intend coming with you the next time you go to see the doctor.'

She looked at him with narrowed eyes. 'Don't you trust me?'

'Julie——'

'All right, all right,' she sighed. 'I'm sorry. And of course you can come with me the next time I visit the doctor.'

'Tomorrow?'

'My appointment isn't for—All right,' she agreed at his stubborn look. 'If you insist.'

'I do.'

As it happened the doctor couldn't give her an appointment until Wednesday, despite Zack's own telephone calls. His waiting for Wednesday morning certainly wasn't done patiently, and several derogatory remarks were made about British doctors.

Julie had been right about Mrs Humphries. Her care of her was almost motherly, and within a couple of days the two of them were firm friends.

'You know I don't like lamb, Mrs Humphries,' Zack complained at dinner on Tuesday evening.

'Mrs Reedman does,' he was informed before the housekeeper bustled off back to her kitchen.

He turned to scowl at Julie. 'You have the woman eating out of your hand!'

Julie ate her meal with quiet enjoyment. 'She's a definite improvement on the housekeeper we had before.' That woman had gone out of her way to treat Julie like a guest instead of her mistress.

Zack ate his own food with less enjoyment, although he made no further comment about the lamb. 'Connie and Ben have been worried about you,' he told her as they drank their coffee in the lounge.

Much to Julie's surprise they had settled down to a

semi-polite existence the last few days; Zack's occasional bouts of temper had soon passed.

'Have they?' she frowned.

'Apparently Connie's been telephoning your flat all week. Ben wondered if I'd heard anything.'

Her mouth twisted. 'And of course you told him I was with you,' she taunted.

He sighed. 'What else would you have had me say?'

Julie shook her head. 'Did you tell him about the baby too?'

'Yes. I felt it would be better coming from me.'

Her cheeks had coloured a delicate pink in her embarrassment. 'Was he pleased?'

'Ecstatic,' Zack revealed dryly. 'You would never think he already had two of his own. I'm surprised Connie hasn't called you,' he added affectionately.

'I've been out all afternoon. Buying baby clothes,' she explained at his censorious look. 'Would you like to see what I've bought?' she offered shyly.

He swallowed hard. 'You really want to show me?' he asked gruffly.

'Babies are for sharing, Zack,' she told him softly.

'Even with me?'

'Especially with you,' she nodded.

'Julie . . .?'

'I'll go and get the things I bought.' She hurried from the room, not trusting the longing in Zack's voice. All that was over between them, she wouldn't allow him to revive it. There was a vast difference between accepting him as the baby's father and accepting him as her husband.

He was staring broodingly into space when she returned to the lounge with the baby-shawl and pram-suit in a beautiful shade of apricot.

'The baby will be born in March, so I thought it

might still be cold then,' she explained the woollen
articles.

'Yes.' Zack looked down at the delicate clothing.
'They're beautiful, Julie,' he said in a husky voice.

She sat down opposite him. 'What are we going
to do about a nursery? I suppose we could convert one
of the bedrooms here, but it's going to be a little
cramped——'

'I thought we could buy a house,' Zack put in quietly.

Julie blinked. 'You did?' It was the first she had
heard of it.

'A flat, especially one in London, is no place to bring
up a child.'

She already knew that, and it had been worrying her.
'You're thinking of moving out of London?'

'I was thinking *we* could move out of London,' he
corrected pointedly.

She frowned. 'But you've always said you have to live
in town.'

'I didn't have a family to think of then. You were
working here, and so was I, London was convenient for
both of us.'

Her mouth twisted. 'And now it isn't?'

He ignored her derision. 'I thought you might like to
live nearer Connie and Ben.'

Her expression brightened. 'I would. But——'

'Then it's settled,' Zack said briskly. 'I've already
contacted an estate agent——'

'Without talking to me first?'

'I only contacted him, Julie. To see if there were any
properties available in that area.'

'And were there?' she enquired stiffly.

'A few,' he nodded. 'I should have the details by the
end of the week.'

Julie was angry, and she wasn't altogether sure why.

A house would be a much more suitable place to bring up a child, and it would be nice to be closer to Connie, Ben, and the children. Maybe it was the fact that Zack hadn't consulted her that bothered her so much, that he had made the decision without even asking her.

'Maybe when you've decided where we're going to live I might be allowed to look at it,' she said tartly.

'Julie——'

She stood up. 'I'll just put these things away,' and she rushed from the room.

Was this how it was to be, how they would live out this lie of a marriage? Was Zack to make all the decisions and she expected to just agree to them? She hadn't been able to accept that sort of marriage last time, and she wouldn't be able to this time either.

She sensed Zack's presence in her room before he spoke, looking up at him challengingly. 'Yes?'

He shrugged his exasperation. 'I have no intention of even looking at a house unless you're with me.'

'No?'

'No!'

'I don't believe you, Zack,' she told him in an unemotional voice. 'I'd like to go to bed now, if you don't mind?'

His expression darkened with concern. 'You're all right?'

'The baby is fine,' she answered wearily. 'I'm just tired.'

'It was you I was asking about,' he scowled.

'Was it?'

'You know it was,' he snapped.

'I——'

A gentle knock sounded on the door. 'Telephone call for you, Mrs Reedman,' the housekeeper told her.

'Connie,' Zack said dryly.

'Probably,' Julie nodded, going back to the lounge.

Connie was so pleased she and Zack were back together, that there was to be a baby, that Julie didn't have the courage to tell her friend the only reason they were back together was *because* of the baby.

Zack had disappeared into his study by the time she managed to get off the telephone, so she went to bed, pretending to be asleep when the door opened quietly about ten minutes later, her eyes remaining firmly closed when she sensed Zack's presence next to the bed.

She almost gave herself away when she felt his hand gently touch her cheek, covering her surprise by turning away from him as if her sleep had been disturbed, holding the tears back from cascading down her cheeks.

'Goodnight, darling,' he murmured huskily several long seconds later.

It seemed to Julie that she must have stopped breathing until she heard the door softly closing as Zack left.

She sat up in the bed, wondering if she could possibly have imagined that moment of tenderness. But she was sure she hadn't, her cheek was still tingling where Zack had touched her.

But why had he touched her? And why had he called her darling?

Dr Frederick told Zack exactly the same as Julie had the next morning—that she was very well, and that the pregnancy was progressing very normally.

'Your wife has been the model expectant mum,' the doctor beamed at them both. 'I wish all women were willing to take the care she has.'

'Julie is very conscious of her health——'

'Of the baby's health,' the doctor corrected briskly. 'Mrs Reedman has been very conscious of the right diet and exercise for your baby, the ante-natal classes she should attend nearer the time.'

'So everything is—normal?' Zack persisted.

'Very much so,' the doctor nodded. 'Of course I can understand your anxiety——'

'Thank you so much for your time, Doctor.' Julie stood up to leave. 'I'm sure my husband feels reassured now. Don't you, Zack?' she looked at him with challenge.

He stood up to shake the doctor's hand. 'You're sure there's nothing more Julie could do to ensure the—safety of the baby?'

'Nothing at all,' the doctor smiled at him indulgently. 'It's just a question of waiting now. And in the meantime you can be sure I'll take good care of her.'

Zack was distant on the drive back to their home, and Julie knew the reason why. 'You still don't trust me, do you?' she sighed.

'I——'

'Don't bother to lie, Zack,' she dismissed. 'You still think I intended sneaking off somewhere and ridding myself of your baby. And what would I have done then? Let me guess,' she said bitterly. 'I would have calmly come back to London, resumed my job, my life? Is that what I would have done, Zack?' she taunted.

'Calm down, Julie——'

'Oh yes, I mustn't get upset, must I? I mustn't do anything to distress the baby! Do you think it's a boy or a girl, Zack? I don't suppose it really matters,' her voice rose shrilly. 'If it's a boy it will probably be a bastard like its father, and if it's a girl it will be a bitch like——'

'No, Julie!' he cut in angrily. 'I won't let you say that. I may be a bastard, a suspicious, cold-hearted bastard, but you are not a bitch. I must have been insane to have said those things to you!' He ran a hand through the darkness of his hair.

'You said you were—insane, I mean.'

'With wanting you! Yes—and heaven help me, I still am,' he groaned. 'The thought of my child growing inside you fills me with wonder and pride.'

Julie had stiffened at his mention of still wanting her. He couldn't mean that, not still.

He turned to her with agonised eyes, and she knew that he did. Zack still wanted her.

'No! No, don't say it,' she shook her head frantically. 'Too much has already been said, done. I won't listen to you any more.'

His expression became shuttered, the light died out of his eyes. 'You feel nothing for me?'

She wouldn't look at him. 'Nothing.'

'I'm sorry,' he said raggedly.

If Mrs Humphries sensed a worsening in the relationship between her master and mistress she gave no indication of it, continuing to fuss over Julie, caring nothing for the scowls of her employer if she should happen to serve a meal he wasn't particularly keen on but which she felt would be good for Julie and the baby.

'I feel like a lodger in my own home,' he told Connie and Ben a few days later; the other couple had been invited over for dinner.

Julie bridled resentfully. 'I'm sure Mrs Humphries doesn't mean to make you feel like that.'

'I know that, darling.' He dropped down beside her on the sofa, his arm going about her shoulders.

She stiffened as he touched her, all contact between them had been kept to the verbal in the last three days. Having him touch her now, when she couldn't stop him, wasn't something she welcomed.

'I like to see the way she takes care of you,' he added

with warm sincerity. 'I often feel like spoiling you myself.'

She looked at him sharply, sensing sarcasm. But it wasn't sarcasm she saw in his face, it was naked desire, his eyes glowed with it. She had seen that look several times the last few days, had seen it, and feared it. Zack really was sorry for all the accusations and cruel things he had said to her when he found out about the baby, and she didn't know if she were strong enough to fight his tenderness, not loving him the way she did.

She had always known that loving a man was like this, more pain than happiness, had thought that three years ago she had escaped its hold on her once and for all. It was worse the second time around, the baby was an added complication she had wanted to avoid at all costs. Now she would never get away, would have to watch while Zack's wanting of now turned to boredom as he searched for a new love to brighten his life.

She had seen it all before, had watched her mother slowly die a little as her father had one woman after another in his life. He had left them so many times in the first ten years of her life that towards the end of that time she had begun to think he *was* the lodger!

It seemed that no matter how many times he left, the cruel things he said, her mother was always willing to take him back. And Julie had been determined that would never happen to her, had refused to have children for that very reason, unwilling to subject any child to the pain she had suffered through her own traumatic and stormy childhood.

And now she was trapped as surely as her mother had been trapped; she loved Zack so much she would have to forgive the other women in his life, would love his child so much she knew she could never leave it— and Zack would never let her take it away with her!

That was one way in which Zack differed from her father. He was possessive over his child, would allow no one else to bring it up but him. Her father hadn't known she was there half the time.

Yes, she was trapped in her own love for Zack and their unborn child, and some of her desperation must have shown in her face, for Zack's arm tightened about her shoulders, a deep frown marring his brow as he looked down at her.

She hastily looked away, knowing how astute Zack could be. Somehow he had never guessed the truth about her reserve when it came to commitment. Probably because she had always told him her father was dead, that both her parents were dead!

Her mother had faded from the world when Julie was eleven years of age, a year after her father had left them for the last time. The doctors said she had died of pneumonia, but Julie knew it had been of a broken heart. Her father had been filing for divorce, had intended marrying the woman he had been living with the last year, and when her mother realised that he really wasn't coming back this time, she had just given up the will to live.

The rest of her life history Zack knew, the years she had spent with her mother's parents, although they too were both dead now. But as far as she knew her father was alive somewhere, and could even have another family by now. She had never felt the least inclination to search him out, just as he had never felt the least bit curious about her.

At the time she had first met Zack, before she realised how important he was going to be in her life, she had told him both her parents were dead. As far as she was concerned it was the truth, her father was emotionally dead to her if not physically. Later it had been too late to correct her statement, so Zack had never been told the truth about her father.

Maybe if he had he would have understood her more, her need to work to maintain her identity, her wish not to bring a child into a potentially dangerous atmosphere, her disillusionment with her parents' marriage warning her that her own marriage could be as disastrous.

'Julie?'

She blinked, looking up at Zack. 'Sorry. I—I was miles away.'

Connie smiled at her. 'I was asking if you'd decided on any names for the baby.'

Colour flooded her cheeks. She and Zack rarely spoke about anything, let alone names for their baby! 'It's a bit early yet,' she said huskily.

'Connie already had the names picked out at three months,' Ben teased his wife. 'I wasn't even consulted!'

Connie playfully punched him in the stomach. 'You couldn't make your mind up,' she protested. 'If I hadn't decided on Nicholas and Suzanne they would probably be called Thingy and Whatshername.'

Ben grinned. 'Probably.'

'I like the name Emily for a girl,' Zack put in softly.

Julie turned sharply to look at him. 'That was my mother's name.'

'Yes,' he nodded.

She wetted her suddenly dry lips. 'I—Thank you.'

'For liking a pretty name?' he teased gently.

'For heaven's sake don't reciprocate and like our father's name!' Ben spluttered with laughter. 'You'll regret it.'

By his humour Julie had a feeling she would, but her

curiosity was aroused. 'What was it?' she rose to Ben's bait.

'Cedric!' he laughed. 'Awful, isn't it?'

'I—well, it——'

'Dreadful,' Zack grinned.

'Yes,' she agreed with a smile.

'Nice evening,' Zack murmured as they came back to the lounge after seeing the other couple off.

'Very nice,' Julie agreed stiltedly. 'I think I'll go to bed now.'

His hand on her arm stopped her leaving. 'Stay and have a drink.'

She avoided looking at him, watching his hand on her arm, his hold very gentle but firm, allowing no chance for escape. 'I think I've had enough for one evening,' she refused.

'Coffee, then?' he persisted.

'Mrs Humphries has gone to bed.'

'I'm perfectly capable of making my wife a cup of coffee,' he teased. 'Please, Julie,' his voice was softly pleading as he sensed her refusal. 'I hardly ever see you. I'm at work all day, we have dinner together, and then you invariably disappear into your bedroom.'

'The doctor told me to rest.'

'I know that,' he nodded. 'But one late evening won't hurt you. Please!'

His complaint that she always went to bed early was a valid one, she knew that. But she felt the less time she spent in his company the less chance he would have of guessing her love for him, a love that seemed to grow stronger every day.

'Sit down,' he encouraged. 'Lie back and put your feet up. Now just sit there until I come back with your coffee.'

She lay back with her eyes closed, too weary to move. She had helped Mrs Humphries with the preparations for the dinner party, and after a week of idleness the extra activity had tired her out. She felt herself drifting off to sleep.

When she heard Zack come back into the room her eyes opened wide with alarm. 'I think maybe I should go to bed after all.' She struggled to sit up, aware of the intimacy of the situation.

'I've made the coffee now,' he pointed out reasonably. 'What happened to you this evening?' he frowned. 'You seemed to drift off for a while.'

'I—It was nothing.'

'No?'

Julie sat forward, picking up the coffee pot, avoiding his probing gaze. 'Would you like some?' she offered, seeing there were two cups on the tray.

'Please,' he nodded, 'Julie——'

'It's too late in the evening for post-mortems, Zack,' she told him in a shrill voice, too tired to parry any move towards intimacy on his part.

'But not too late completely?'

She swallowed hard, seeing the determination in his face. 'I think we're better off as we are.'

'Better as we are!' he scorned, coming down on his haunches beside her and taking her shaking hands in his. 'You can't mean that, Julie,' he pleaded.

'I do.'

'But we're living like strangers——'

'We are strangers,' her eyes flashed. 'What do you know about me, Zack? Really know about me?'

He frowned at her vehemence. 'What sort of question is that? We're married——'

'But what do you really know about me? You rushed our courtship, made me marry you after only knowing you a month. And you said yourself that we were only together fifty-six days out of our year of marriage.'

'I didn't need to be with you to know I loved you!'

'You can't love someone you don't know!'

'I knew you, Julie.' He wrenched her chin up, forcing her to look at him. 'I *know* you. And I can't continue to live like this. I want you beside me at night, Julie. I want to hold you, love you——'

'No!' she wrenched away from him, getting to her feet. 'No!' She turned, falling over the stool he had put at her feet, and landed heavily on the floor, the breath knocked from her body.

'Julie!' Zack's cry came out hoarse. 'Oh, Julie!'

'Get me to hospital, Zack,' she groaned, her eyes closing. 'Oh please God don't let it happen again. Not again!' she choked.

'Again?' Zack echoed sharply. 'What do you mean? Julie!'

She couldn't answer him. Blackness shadowed over her as she lost consciousness of the world.

CHAPTER NINE

'JUST a faint,' the doctor assured her at the hospital.

'The—the baby?' She lay on the examination couch, her expression anxious.

'The baby is fine,' he patted her hand reassuringly. 'Although I'm going to keep you in for a couple of days.'

'Then the baby isn't all right!' Julie struggled to sit up. 'Tell me——'

'The baby is unharmed,' he soothed. 'Really. I just think a couple of days' rest wouldn't do you any harm. Now I'd better let your husband in. He's been prowling the waiting-room for the last half an hour.'

'Oh no, Zack! What had she said to him after that fall? What had she given away? One look at Zack's harsh face when the doctor brought him in showed her that she had said too much.

'The doctor tells me you're both all right,' he said distantly.

'Yes,' she looked at him with apprehensive eyes.

'A couple of days' rest and Mrs Reedman can come home,' the doctor told them cheerfully, finishing writing up his notes. 'The fall was a shock to her, and in the circumstances I'm sure you can understand our caution.'

Zack looked at him with bleak eyes. 'Yes.'

The doctor stood up. 'I'll leave you alone for a few minutes now, then we'll get Mrs Reedman to her room.'

'Thank you,' Zack said deeply.

'There really is no need to worry,' the doctor assured

them. 'The admission is just a precaution on my part.'
He left them alone.

Julie looked up at Zack, dreading the next few
minutes with him. She had given herself away
irrevocably, and Zack would, quite rightly, demand an
explanation.

'Zack——'

'You lost my child once before.' He spoke as if he
hadn't heard her, pain etched into his harsh features.

She swallowed hard. 'Yes.'

'When?'

She turned her head away, staring sightlessly at the
lemon-painted walls. 'It must be obvious—after I left
you,' she said woodenly.

'Why didn't you tell me?' he rasped. 'Why keep
something like that to yourself? Unless the child wasn't
mine?' His voice deepened with suspicion.

She looked at him now, her eyes glittering deeply
green. 'How dare you say that?' she choked. 'How
could you——'

'Because you didn't tell me!' His fingers bit into her
arms as he shook her. 'Why keep something like that to
yourself if the child were mine?'

He looked demonic in that moment, totally out of
control, accusation in the coldness of his eyes.

And Julie hated him for it, hated him for the distrust
he didn't even try to hide. An hour ago he had wanted
to make love to her, his own words were 'to *love* her',
and now he was as good as accusing her of becoming
pregnant by another man, of losing this mythical
someone else's baby.

'You're right, Zack,' she scorned, more hurt than she
would ever allow him to see. 'The baby wasn't yours.'

He seemed to go grey. 'It wasn't?'

She looked at him with cold eyes. 'What's the matter,

Zack? You seem surprised. Wasn't that what you wanted to hear?'

'You know very well it wasn't!' He thrust her away from him. 'Is it the truth?'

'No,' she said wearily.

'No . . .?' he rasped.

'Of course not,' she sighed, defeated. 'The baby was yours, and I lost it.'

'Then why lie?'

'Because I hate you!' she told him vehemently. 'You're so quick to throw out accusations, to blame everyone but yourself.'

'Myself?' he echoed with a frown. 'Are you saying I was to blame for the loss of the baby?'

She shook her head dully. 'It just happened. No one can control these things.'

'Why did no one know? Connie——'

'Had no idea,' she defended her friend. 'It doesn't take long to lose a baby, Zack. Just a matter of minutes, in fact,' she recalled bitterly. 'And a few days later you're fit to go back out into the world.' She looked at him with pained eyes. 'Only inside you aren't. Inside you're still hurting, still grieving. As I still am. I wanted that baby, wanted it badly.' She was no longer looking at him, talking softly to herself, realising for the first time that it was true. She *had* wanted that first baby badly—as she wanted this one.

'Julie——'

The fight was back in her eyes as she looked at him. 'No more words, Zack, they don't mean an awful lot on their own. I lost your baby once before, but this one, *this one* I intend holding on to. Even if I have to stay married to you to do so,' she added cuttingly.

Zack seemed to blanch. 'You really do hate me.'

'What did you expect?' she scorned. 'In the last three

months you've made love to me, callously left me without a word the next morning, proposed an affair with me, and now you're forcing me to live with you. What do you expect me to do, Zack, love you?'

'No,' he said wearily. 'I—I'll let them get you to your room now. I'll be back to see you tomorrow.'

Those few days Julie spent in hospital changed her relationship with Zack completely. When she returned home Zack was no longer the angry, accusing man he had been, nor did he show any signs of physical attraction to her. In fact, as the weeks progressed he became more of a friend to her.

Admittedly it was an uneasy friendship, treated tentatively at first by Julie, and then with growing confidence as the weeks turned into months and Zack's coolly concerned manner remained constant.

They finally found a house to their liking about three miles from where Connie and Ben lived, and once the decorators had been in and they were actually able to move in Connie and the children became regular daytime visitors.

To all intents and purposes the marriage was a real one to outsiders. Zack's tender care was in evidence at all times, and only Mrs Humphries and the daily woman they had hired to help in the house knew of their separate sleeping arrangements. It was quite easy to make the baby an excuse for that, especially as Mrs Humphries was aware of Julie's short stay in hospital.

But Julie was dissatisfied, and she knew Zack wasn't really happy. Not by word or deed did he show this, coming home from work to talk about the day's events like any other husband, but occasionally she would look up and find him watching her, a deep hunger in his eyes, a hunger that he would quickly mask.

If he was still seeing Teresa Barr, or any other woman for that matter, then she didn't know when. All his days were spent at work, all his evenings at home, so if there was a woman in his life he didn't see her very often.

Towards the end of her eighth month of pregnancy she began to prepare the nursery. She had been too afraid to before this, not wanting to tempt fate. Mrs Humphries helped, enjoying it immensely, and the two of them had great fun picking out the wallpaper and curtains.

Zack had declined helping her choose them, seeming to spend more and more time in his study in the evenings.

'Is the travelling too much for you?' she finally asked him.

'Mm?' He looked up abstractedly.

Julie frowned at the deep lines etched beside his nose and mouth. They hadn't been there a few months ago. 'You seem tired, withdrawn,' she said carefully.

'I'm fine—really.'

'The travelling——'

'Is no bother,' he dismissed, the evening newspaper still open in front of him—as it had been for the last half an hour.

'Then work——'

'No heavier than usual.'

She bit her lip worriedly. 'Then what is it?'

He looked at her with vague grey eyes. 'What's what?'

'Zack, what's wrong?' She stood up, her body heavy in this last month of pregnancy, the thick woollen dress exactly matching the green of her eyes. 'You've been so quiet since Christmas.'

It had been a lovely family gathering at Connie and

Ben's, with obscure uncles and aunts putting in an appearance too. Only Zack had remained removed from the family fun, and he had remained that way ever since.

'I've been busy at work——'

'You just said it was no heavier than usual.'

He glared at her with an impatient frown. 'What is this, Julie, an inquisition?'

She flinched at his scornful tone. 'I'm just concerned about you.'

'Why?' he rasped.

'I just am!' she snapped back.

He shrugged, carefully folding the newspaper before putting it on the coffee-table. 'If you must know, I felt—guilty, about deceiving everyone. The whole family think we're ecstatically happy together.'

Julie turned away. 'I'm sorry,' she said quietly.

'So am I. I'm sorry I ever forced myself on you, sorry I—Sorry I—Oh Julie, I'm just sorry for everything!' He stood up to storm out of the room.

Julie hurried after him. 'Zack!'

He turned halfway up the stairs, his expression remote. 'Yes?'

She wetted her lips nervously. 'I—Where are you going?'

'Bed.'

She blinked. 'But it's only nine-thirty!'

Zack sighed heavily. 'I'm not fit company tonight, Julie. Surely you can see that?'

'Is it something I've done?' she persisted.

'No,' he said ruefully. 'Something we *haven't* done. In a long time.'

Colour flooded her cheeks as his meaning became clear to her. 'I'm hardly in any condition for that,' she derided to cover her embarrassment.

'I didn't necessarily mean sex, Julie,' he dismissed scathingly. 'Sometimes at night, I have this urge to hold you, to maybe feel our child moving inside you. Sometimes—sometimes it almost drives me crazy!' He ran up the rest of the stairs, and his bedroom door slammed a few seconds later.

Mrs Humphries appeared from the kitchen, a worried frown to her brow. 'Is there anything wrong? I thought I heard shouting.'

'Just Mr Reedman calling to me from upstairs,' Julie dismissed with a tight smile.

'If you're sure . . .?'

'Yes, I'm sure.' She forced her smile to be brighter. 'Mr Reedman and I are having an early night tonight, Mrs Humphries, so you can lock up if you like.'

She made her way slowly up the stairs, her movements slow and laboured. Once in her room she went through her usual nightly ritual of cleansing her face, her movements mechanical, her thoughts on other things.

Poor Zack, he had only been voicing a hunger she often had herself, even more so as the time for the baby to be born neared. She often felt she needed his strength, just his calm presence to reassure her. And tonight was no exception. Knowing that Zack felt the same way only made her own longing worse.

And why shouldn't they sleep together, share a bed at least? They were married, and as she had already pointed out, she was in no condition for the physical side of their marriage.

All was quiet in Zack's room as she made her way across the passage; his room was opposite hers, and the door was firmly closed. Maybe he would be asleep, if he was she wouldn't disturb him.

The light was off inside his room, only his still figure

beneath the bedclothes evidence of his presence. She turned to leave.

'Julie . . .?'

When she looked back he was sitting up in bed, the light from the passageway outside his room showing his bare chest, the puzzled look on his face as he stared at her. 'I—er——' she wetted her lips in her nervousness. 'I—wondered if you might like some—company.' Heavens, how feeble that sounded!

He flicked on the bedside lamp. 'You can't sleep?'

She shrugged, her hands together awkwardly in front of her, unwittingly emphasising her condition. 'I haven't tried yet,' she told him softly.

'Then why——? I don't understand,' he frowned his puzzlement.

'Zack, I get lonely too sometimes,' her voice pleaded for his understanding. 'And the nights can seem very long then,' she added huskily.

For long timeless minutes he continued to look at her, then he slowly threw back the bedclothes beside him. 'Come and join me?' he invited softly.

Julie hesitated only a moment, then she turned to him as she lay on the bed, letting him tuck the bedclothes firmly about her. His arms came about her, pulling her into the hardness of his bare chest, the rest of him just as naked.

'Mm, heaven!' he breathed into her hair, reaching out to switch off the lamp.

He was right, it was heaven. It was also torture too! It was the first time in months he had so much as touched her, so it was the first time she had realised the inconvenience of being eight months pregnant when being held in a man's arms. It was virtually impossible to get close to him!

Zack was aware of it too, and laughed softly. 'Maybe

you should turn the other way,' he suggested teasingly.
'At least that way I could cuddle you spoon-fashion.'

'In a minute,' she nodded. At the moment she was
just luxuriating in the pleasure of being held, of feeling Zack's strength become her own. All the fears of
the birth of the baby receded when she was held
close to Zack like this, her natural fear of the
unknown evaporating in his quiet self-confidence. Zack
would take care of her, she didn't doubt that for a
moment.

Some time in the night they did cuddle spoon-
fashion. Julie was aware of Zack's warmth as she half
woke towards morning, could hear his deep even
breathing and knew he slept peacefully, that there
would be none of the working in the night that she had
often been aware of lately. Zack's movements downstairs had occasionally disturbed her.

She slept soundlessly herself, waking up mid-morning
to find herself alone, Zack having gone to work long
ago. But she felt none of the rejection she had felt the
last time they had slept together and she had woken to
find him gone, feeling only a closeness towards him, a
bond that the baby was forging between them without
them even being aware of it.

Her feelings of contentment took her through the day
with a happy smile on her face, and she greeted Zack
warmly when he arrived home early that evening. The
flowers he gave her brought a glow to her cheeks, and
for once their evening was spent in harmonious
relaxation, the conversation spontaneous and not
forced.

As if by tacit agreement they both went to Zack's
bedroom that night. There were no questions, no
answers, just mutual consent to their new sleeping
arrangements.

And so it was that when the baby decided to be born two weeks early Zack was lying in the bed beside her, his deep breathing once again telling her of his contented sleep, his arm about her thickened waistline.

'Zack?' She shook that arm gently so as not to alarm him.

'Mm?'

'Zack!' she repeated sharply as he made no effort to wake up but simply cuddled more comfortably against her.

He was instantly awake, shooting up into a sitting position. 'I—What is it?' he blinked dazedly.

'The baby.'

'The baby?' He still looked sleep-drugged. 'You didn't wake me up to tell me it moved?' He sounded incredulous.

'Zack, please wake up! I——' She gasped as a painful contraction shot through her body. 'Time them, Zack,' she instructed him. 'I have to let the hospital know when we call how quickly the pains are coming.'

He was completely awake now, falling out of bed rather than getting out, pulling clothes haphazardly out of the wardrobe.

'Zack, what are you doing?' she asked as he put on two completely different shoes.

'Mm—what?' He looked down, hastily changing the shoes for a matching pair. 'I don't know what I am doing,' he muttered as he had to take his shirt off, somehow having put it on inside-out. 'What are you smiling at?' he asked suspiciously, his movements slowing. 'This isn't some sort of joke, is it? A sort of dress rehearsal?'

As a 'dress' rehearsal it would have been a disaster! 'No,' Julie giggled.

'A false alarm?' he asked hopefully.

'No,' Julie shook her head, still smiling.

'You really are having the baby now?'

'Yes,' she nodded happily.

'Then what are you smiling about?'

'You,' she sobered. 'I always thought you would be calm and collected when the time came, and instead you're acting like someone in a comedy show,' she laughed again.

'I've never been a father before!' he scowled.

'It shows,' she teased him.

'Julie—Another one?' His threatening tone turned to one of concern as he saw her wince.

'Yes,' she gasped.

'Five minutes,' he murmured. 'I'm not even going to call the hospital, I'm just taking you straight there!'

Considering what a busy place a hospital was during the day it had a strangely eerie feeling at night. Zack's footsteps echoed hollowly in the corridor as Julie was wheeled from Emergency to the delivery ward.

'If you would like to wait outside, Mr Reedman.'

'I'm staying,' he told the nurse firmly as she tried to usher him out of the room.

'But, Mr Reedman——'

'Julie?' he looked at her sharply.

Julie saw the anxiety in his face, her heart contracting. 'He's staying,' she told the nurse huskily.

And he did stay. For the next eight and a half hours he didn't leave her side, talking to her soothingly during the calm times, letting her squeeze the blood from his fingers during the painful ones.

It was during that eight and a half hours that she knew the bond between them to be cemented for ever, that her life and Zack's would always remain one, that the baby would add to, not detract from the love she felt towards him. And which he felt for her, she was sure of it.

When their daughter was born she cried in Zack's arms, felt his tears mingle with her own as the baby was placed in her arms seconds later, love overflowing between them as they both gazed down in awe at their beautiful daughter.

The doctor smiled at them. 'No problems this time, Mrs Reedman,' he assured her. 'Everything went normally.'

She had known that. Everything had been different from last time; her pregnancy had been quite an easy one, any extra precautions she had taken had been because of Zack and the doctor. But little Emily was worth it, and helped banish the hurt for that other little daughter who hadn't been allowed to live.

Zack left a short time later, with a promise to come back later in the evening. He looked as weary as she felt, and she only hoped he managed to get some sleep this afternoon.

Julie rested herself, and by the time she woke up she had two bouquets and some telegrams. The baby was still sleeping peacefully in her crib next to the bed, seemingly exhausted too. For a moment Julie gazed with wonder at the perfection of the child she had brought into the world, at the thatch of red hair so like her own, the skin a delicate pink, the little hands screwed up into fists, as if Emily would dearly love to punch the person who had dragged her out of her warm cocoon into a world that seemed to consist of bright light and loud noises.

Feeding the baby for the first time was an awkward as well as a pleasurable experience, and she blushed scarlet as Zack entered the room in the middle of her first efforts to coax Emily into feeding.

She quickly looked down at the baby, avoiding his suddenly fierce gaze. 'I—She doesn't seem to want to feed.'

'She will,' he assured her, coming to stand at the side of the bed. 'If she has any sense,' he added provocatively.

Julie's blush deepened. 'I think that's enough for now.' She cradled the baby to her as she tried to fasten her nightgown back into place.

'Here, let me.' Zack held out his arms for his daughter.

She gave Emily to him, hastily straightening her clothing, watching with pleasure the tenderness on Zack's face as he gazed down at the baby.

His eyes were almost black as he looked up at her. 'You never told me you were going to feed the baby yourself.'

'You never asked me.' Her blush deepened.

'No, I suppose not. Connie sends her love, she'll be in to see you tomorrow.'

'Thank you,' she nodded. 'You look rested,' she added.

'I managed to get a couple of hours. I suppose I'll have to get used to sleepless nights now.'

'Yes,' she agreed ruefully, thinking how right he looked holding Emily.

'She's beautiful, Julie,' he told her throatily.

She flushed her pleasure. 'You really think so?'

'Did you doubt it?' he teased.

'I—I couldn't be sure.'

'Then be sure.' His voice was firm. 'I couldn't have asked for a more beautiful daughter.'

'She looks like me,' Julie said shyly.

'Exactly.'

'Zack——'

'She's beautiful, Julie,' he repeated softly. 'I think she just fell asleep,' he whispered in an awed voice.

'Probably,' she nodded. 'She's been trying to guzzle for some time.'

'So I saw,' he drawled.

'Put her in the crib, Zack!' Her voice was sharp in her embarrassment.

He did so, carefully, before moving to unpack the bag he had brought with him. 'Magazines, books, chocolates, drink,' he listed the items as he placed them on the side.

'I got your flowers, Zack.' Julie looked at the beautiful vase of red roses. 'Thank you.'

'Julie, I hope you aren't going to be annoyed,' he avoided her gaze, 'but as you prepared the room next to yours for the nursery, and as I like sleeping beside you, I've moved my things into your room.' He looked at her almost challengingly now, as if expecting her objection.

She met his gaze unflinchingly. 'Did you find enough room for all your things?' she asked calmly.

'Er—yes.' He looked startled. 'You mean you don't mind?'

'Not in the least. I was wondering how we were going to manage once the baby had been born.'

'Julie——'

'Mr Reedman,' the doctor appeared in the doorway, 'I can spare the time for that chat now.'

'Yes, of course,' he nodded. 'I'll be with you in two minutes.'

'Zack, what's wrong?' she demanded worriedly once the doctor had gone. 'There's nothing wrong with Emily——'

'Nothing at all,' he soothed. 'I just wanted a few words with the doctor to check that you're all right. I don't want to take any chances. I'll be back in a moment, darling.' He kissed her lightly on the lips.

But he wasn't back in a moment, or in the next hour. In fact, he didn't come back at all.

CHAPTER TEN

JULIE'S first thought when Zack didn't return as he had said he would was that he had been delayed by the doctor. The nurse who came in to take Emily to the nursery for her nappy change soon put paid to that idea.

'Mr Reedman left the hospital about fifteen minutes ago,' the nurse told her in a cheerful voice, wheeling Emily out of the room in her crib.

Julie's second thoughts were ones of bewilderment. He had only just arrived, surely he hadn't left again so soon—and without saying goodbye to her?

But as the minutes ticked away and visiting time came to an end she knew he had gone, that he wasn't coming back again tonight. Her telephone call to the house was answered by Mrs Humphries.

'Is Mr Reedman there?' she asked anxiously.

'Why, of course, Mrs Reedman,' the housekeeper seemed puzzled by the question.

'Could I talk to him, please?'

'Of course, I'll get him. And congratulations, Mrs Reedman,' the woman added warmly. 'Eight pounds is a nice healthy size.'

'Yes,' Julie answered shyly.

'I'll go and get Mr Reedman.'

She waited impatiently for Zack to come to the telephone. At least he was all right, not hurt as she had expected in her worst fears. Although why he had left the hospital so suddenly she had no idea.

'Er—Could I possibly take a message?' The housekeeper returned to the telephone a few minutes later.

She frowned. 'Isn't Zack there?'

'I—Yes. But——'

'Then why hasn't he come to the telephone?' she asked sharply.

'Because he—he——'

'Mrs Humphries, is Zack ill?'

'No. No, he isn't ill. Not exactly.' The housekeeper sounded uncomfortable.

'Then what is it?' Julie demanded to know.

'He's in the study. With the door locked,' Mrs Humphries sounded really flustered now. 'And he says he doesn't want to speak to you,' the last she added in a scandalised voice.

'Not speak to me . . .?'

'I'm sorry, Mrs Reedman. I tried to reason with him,' she explained the reason she had been gone so long. 'But he refused to open the door. I—I think he's been drinking,' she added tentatively.

Julie frowned, not understanding this at all. What on earth was wrong with Zack? 'Thank you, Mrs Humphries.' She rang off, her puzzlement now a tangible thing.

Why had Zack left like that? What had she done to make him leave without even saying goodbye? And why was he drinking? Could it be that he finally knew the truth and couldn't forgive her?

Her agitation must have been evident to the nurse who brought Emily in to say goodnight. The first two nights of her stay in hospital were baby-free as she got all the sleep she could after the birth.

'What's wrong, Mrs Reedman?' the nurse asked concernedly when she came back from the nursery, eyeing Julie's flushed cheeks worriedly.

Julie's movements were agitated. 'Is Dr Bessell still on duty?'

'He was in the office a moment ago——'

'Could you get him for me?'

'Are you feeling unwell?'

'I'm feeling fine,' she said shrilly. 'I just have to talk to the doctor.'

The nurse hurried away, coming back a few minutes later to shake her head. 'I'm afraid he's already left for the night.'

'Then I have to leave.' Julie threw back the bedclothes, swinging her legs to the floor.

'Mrs Reedman!' The nurse rushed over to stop her. 'You mustn't get out of bed yet.'

In actual fact she had begun to feel dizzy as soon as her feet touched the ground, but she had to see Zack, had to find out if it was the past that had driven this wedge between them once again. 'I have to go——'

'You have to stay in bed.'

'I have to see my husband!'

'I'm sure he'll be in tomorrow,' the young nurse soothed. 'Couldn't it wait until then?'

Julie doubted very much that Zack would be in tomorrow or any other day, not if what she suspected were right. She might never see him again! But the nurse was right, she did have to stay in bed, the world was beginning to swing on its axis.

'That's better!' The bedclothes were smoothed over her as she lay back among the pillows. 'Now try and get some sleep, Mrs Reedman. The doctor will be in to see you first thing in the morning.'

Strangely she did sleep, the disturbed night of yesterday and the birth of Emily seeming to catch up with her. She awoke with a start, finding it was the lusty sound of her daughter's lungs that had interrupted her sleep. The next few minutes were taken up with feeding

Emily, more successfully this time, and the tiny baby fell asleep halfway through the feeding, a look of contentment on her face.

Julie had just laid the baby back down when the doctor came into the room, coming straight over to sit on the side of her bed.

'Nurse Grove left a message for me to come and see you immediately. I got to the hospital—even before I've had my breakfast,' he added teasingly. 'What seems to be the trouble?'

She bit her lip nervously. 'My husband—what did you talk to him about yesterday?'

He frowned at the question. 'You, mostly.'

'I—Could you be more specific?'

The doctor shrugged. 'Your husband, quite naturally, wanted to be assured as to your own health.'

'Yes?'

He raised his eyebrows in puzzlement. 'I reassured him.'

Julie bit her lip. 'What else did you tell him?'

'Nothing. Mrs Reedman, what's wrong?'

She looked at him pleadingly. 'I have to know exactly what you said to my husband, what you told him.'

He frowned. 'I'm not sure I can remember.'

'Please try,' she encouraged huskily, her intent gaze never leaving his face.

'Well,' he seemed to consider, 'I recall we talked about how well the birth went, how there should be no problem with your having other children, that the miscarriage you had last time was an accident.'

'Yes?' her voice sharpened.

'That's all,' he shrugged.

'Did you tell my husband—what sort of accident it was?' She held her breath as she waited for his answer.

'I don't—I remember now, he asked to see the notes. Of course I refused, but I did assure him that it was very unlikely it would happen again.'

'Thank you.' A dull throbbing had begun behind her eyes. Zack knew. After all this time, he finally knew the truth. That *was* the reason he didn't want to see her, the reason he found a whisky bottle better company.

Oh dear heaven, what was she going to do now! Talk to Zack—she had to talk to Zack! Mrs Humphries once again answered the telephone.

'Mr Reedman isn't here,' she told Julie.

'Not—there?'

'No,' the housekeeper confirmed. 'His room hasn't been slept in.'

'Have you looked in the study?'

'Oh, Mrs Reedman,' the housekeeper came back a few minutes later, sounding very agitated, 'he's in there, slumped over his desk. He—he looks awful, Mrs Reedman! And he didn't even wake up when I shook him.'

'Don't worry, Mrs Humphries,' Julie smoothed. 'I'll deal with it. Just stay calm.' She had to get out of here, she really had to this time.

'What on earth are you doing?' The same nurse as yesterday came in just as Julie was finishing dressing.

In actual fact she felt a little lightheaded; she had never realised how weak having a baby made you feel. But she had to go to Zack, had to talk to him, to make him realise . . .

'Mrs Reedman——'

'I'll be back soon,' she promised.

'I'm going to get the doctor,' and the nurse hurried off.

They were back within minutes, the doctor adding his argument to the nurse's.

Julie's eyes flashed as she waited for him to finish. 'You can say what you like, Dr Bessell, but I have to leave.'

'You aren't well enough——'

'I have to see my husband.'

'Call him instead,' the doctor reasoned.

'I have to *see* him!' she insisted heatedly.

He looked at her with frustrated anger. 'All right,' he finally sighed defeat in the face of her stubbornness. 'I'll take you.'

'Doctor——'

'If I don't take her,' the doctor explained to the nurse, 'Mrs Reedman will leave the hospital anyway. Won't you?' he quirked an eyebrow at Julie.

'Yes,' she nodded determinedly. 'Please take good care of Emily for me,' she requested huskily of the nurse.

'I gather this urgent request to see your husband has something to do with my conversation with him last night?' the doctor remarked on the drive.

'Yes.' Her gaze was intent on the road ahead, wishing the miles away.

'I hope I didn't say anything out of turn?'

'No,' she shook her head. 'This is just—something I should have discussed with Zack long ago.'

Mrs Humphries went into a complete panic when Julie entered the house.

'Is my husband still in the study?' she wanted to know.

'Well, yes. But——'

'Give Dr Bessell some coffee, please,' she requested the housekeeper. 'Breakfast too, if he would like it.'

Her stomach gave a sickening lurch before she determinedly opened the door to the study. Zack was still slumped over the desk, a greyness to his face that she had never seen before.

She went down on her haunches beside him, shaking him gently. 'Zack? Zack darling, please wake up.'

He stirred, his eyes opening momentarily, his shoulder stiffening beneath her hand as he looked down at her, his eyes becoming wide and alert now, the navy blue trousers and light blue shirt creased from where he had slept in them. 'Julie . . .?' he blinked dazedly.

Her heart contracted. 'Yes.'

'Dear heaven!' he rasped, sitting back. 'Julie?' he frowned his uncertainty. 'You shouldn't be here,' he gasped. 'You should be in hospital, not here.'

'You wouldn't come to me . . .' she trailed off pointedly.

His face became harsh. 'You know why,' he said bitterly.

She put her hand on his arm. 'Zack——'

He stood up forcefully, pain etched into his face, his hands clenching and unclenching at his sides. 'How can you even bear to talk to me, Julie? How can you *want* to! Dear heaven, it was me all the time! All the time I said those vicious things to you you knew it was really my fault. *I* killed our baby,' he groaned, his face buried in his hands.

'No——'

'Yes!' he looked at her with tears on his cheeks. 'Don't deny it, Julie, because I know the truth now. You lost our baby the same night I forced myself on you. Forced!' he scorned the description bitterly. 'I *raped* you. And you lost our baby because of it.'

It was the truth—the truth, as she knew he must one day discover. But not now, now when it had seemed happiness had been within their grasp!

The doctor had explained the need for care in the first months of that pregnancy three years ago, and it had been advice she intended taking. The anticipation of telling Zack about the baby had kept her in a state of excitement all day. What a first wedding anniversary present it would be for him!

And then had come the call from her editor, the unexpected trip to Germany. And Zack's even more unexpected burst of uncontrollable anger. She had tried to reason with him, had pleaded, and in the end it had been in vain. She hadn't gone to Germany, instead she had lost the baby, so easily, had suffered little pain, while inside she had been crying all the tears that had refused to be released.

But they were released now, as she cried for both Zack and herself, for the baby that should have been an older sister for Emily.

'How you must hate me,' Zack choked, his shoulders shaking as he too cried.

'I *love* you, Zack,' she told him with feeling. 'I always have, and I always will. And there's a certain young lady at the hospital who loves you too.'

He swallowed hard. 'Emily . . .'

She rested her head on his chest, her arms about his waist. 'Yes, Emily. We lost one child, Zack, yes. But——'

'I killed her, Julie!' he rasped. 'I *killed* her.'

'No,' she shook her head. 'They told me, the doctors, that there was something wrong with the pregnancy anyway.'

'Emily——'

'Is fine,' she reassured him softly, smoothing the frown from his brow. 'The other baby—it was just a freak of nature, nothing you or I did. You didn't kill her, Zack. I lost her that night, yes, but the doctor said I would probably have miscarried later anyway. God just decided she would be better off with him, darling.'

'You really believe that?' he asked shakily.

Until this moment she hadn't really thought about it, but nature had a way of continuing the life cycle as it saw fit. That was something she did believe.

'Yes,' she nodded with certainty, 'I really believe it.'

He swallowed hard, the pain still in his eyes. 'Did you—did you just tell me you *love* me?'

'Yes. And I'm going to tell you again in a minute.' Once again she rested her head on his chest, hearing the loud tattoo of his heartbeat. 'We never said it enough, Zack, never dared say it, I think. But things are going be different from now on.'

'From now on?' His chest rumbled beneath her ear.

'Oh yes,' she looked up at him unflinchingly. 'Emily and I are here to stay, so you might as well get used to the idea.'

'You really want to continue living with me?'

'I not only want it, I'm going to do it. And as soon as the doctor gives me the go-ahead I'm going to *show* you just how much I love you.'

'But, Julie——'

'Zack, I love you, I love you, I love you!' It was as if something had been released within her, a rein no longer put on her love so that she could pull it back if it looked as if she were going to be hurt. If you couldn't love wholeheartedly, unreservedly, then there was no point in loving at all, she could see that now. And in future she intended holding nothing back, not a single part of her love.

Zack eyed her nervously, like a child who has chocolate within its reach and is afraid to take it in case he gets his hand smacked. 'Julie . . .?'

'I love you, love you, love you,' she punctuated her words with light kisses over his throat and jaw.

'And God knows I love you!' his arms tightened

about her. 'I've always loved you. But I never thought, didn't imagine, you could love me as much. You always seemed to hold back.'

Julie began to tell him, haltingly at first, and then more rapidly as the words spilled out, about her fear of loving anyone as much as she loved him, of her parents' unhappy marriage, her father's infidelity, her mother's despair.

He was even paler by the time she had finished. 'And you thought I would do that to you?' he groaned.

'I was afraid to give you the chance,' she admitted softly. 'But that's over now, Zack. Emily and I need you so badly, darling.' She looked up at him adoringly.

'For better or worse, Julie, you've got me,' he groaned into her throat. 'It's never been any different. You, always you.'

'And Teresa?' she teased lightly.

'A beautiful woman, but not you. Even when we were apart it was still you.'

As Mrs Tibbles had said. Dear Mrs Tibbles, how right she was. When you loved as she and Zack loved, as Mrs Tibbles and her Harry loved, then you were together even when you were apart.

'No more partings, Zack,' she answered him huskily. 'Never any more.'

He smoothed her hair from her brow. 'Do you know the moment I knew it had to be you and no one else?'

'Tell me,' she encouraged softly.

'It was the hijacking,' he rasped, remembered pain tightening his mouth. 'I'd decided that Teresa would make me a suitable wife, that divorcing you was the only answer. And then I found out you were one of the hostages on that plane! I went through hell trying to get you off there.'

Her eyes widened. '*You* tried to get me off?'

He nodded. 'I went to every official I could to try and get an end to the siege. In the end the most, or least, I could do was give them the money they wanted.'

'But that was millions!' she gasped.

'Yes,' he breathed raggedly. 'I would have given them everything I had to get you off that plane. I even offered myself in exchange, but I was told that if they realised they had my wife on board you could be used as leverage.'

'That's why you were in America!'

'Yes,' he sighed. 'Why I had to content myself with letting Connie and Ben take care of you, when I wanted to do it. We had to go through all the paperwork, the formalities. But when I got back to England I was determined to see you again, so I arranged that dinner party for our anniversary. When you decided not to come with Connie and Ben I decided to come and see you at the house. I *had* to see you. One look at your face when I walked into the house was enough to tell me you hated the sight of me!'

'No!'

'Oh yes,' Zack nodded. 'But I couldn't stop wanting you. Those threats of divorce never got any further than issuing the papers. I thought maybe if it looked official that you would somehow realise you still loved me too. It didn't work.'

'And the affair?'

'I was going crazy, Julie,' he groaned. 'I needed you so badly. You'd always said that an affair between us would have been less complicated. By that time I was willing to take you any way I could get you.'

'There have never been any affairs, Zack,' she told him huskily. 'Not with Alec, and not with Steve, not with anyone else either. Although there is someone I'd like to have an affair with,' she added lightly. 'A lifelong love affair.'

'Yes?' he was tense.

'I love you, Zack,' she breathed softly, gazing up at him adoringly. 'I love you so much.'

His mouth moving druggingly over hers stopped all further conversation, the giving and receiving of unreserved love taking both their breaths away. 'I love you, Julie,' he murmured against her earlobe. 'I'll always love you, want you, need you. Never doubt that.'

'I won't. I——'

A knock sounded briskly on the door. 'Mrs Reedman?' the doctor called out to her. 'I really must insist that you go back to the hospital now.'

'Oh, yes,' Zack groaned, looking down at her concernedly. 'Are you all right?'

'I'm fine,' Julie smiled up at him.

'Mrs Reedman!' the doctor called again.

Zack sighed, giving a rueful grin. 'We'd better do as he says. After all, we have a lifetime ahead of us.' He sobered.

Yes, they had a lifetime, for them a lifetime love affair.

HARLEQUIN'S SPECIAL LASAGNA

One of the dishes Juliet and Steve probably enjoyed at Mario's, "a quiet little Italian restaurant in the back streets of London," is lasagna, a popular pasta. If you'd like to try this delicious Italian food at home, here's Harlequin's own special recipe (enough for eight). Enjoy!

What you need:

1 lb. ground beef	1 tbsp. parsley
½ lb. sausage meat, chopped	½ tsp. salt
¼ lb. salami, chopped	2 tsp. oregano
1 medium onion, chopped	dash cayenne
1 green pepper, chopped	dash pepper
1 28-oz. tin tomatoes	1 lb. mozzarella cheese, grated
2 5½-oz. tins tomato paste	⅔ cup Parmesan cheese, grated
dash Worcestershire sauce	1 cup ricotta cheese
½ tsp. sugar	2 eggs, beaten
½ tsp basil	1 lb. lasagna noodles

What to do:

Brown meats in large saucepan (no oil necessary), then drain off fat. Add next 12 ingredients, bring to a boil, then simmer, uncovered, for approximately 2 hours, until sauce is very thick.

Cook lasagna noodles according to package directions. Lightly grease a 9 x 12 in. casserole dish. Combine eggs, ricotta and ½ cup Parmesan. Place a single layer of noodles in bottom of casserole, then a layer of sauce, then a layer of mozzarella. Make another layer of noodles, then a layer using all of the ricotta mixture, then some sauce, then some noodles. End with a layer of mozzarella, noodles and sauce. Sprinkle remaining Parmesan over all, cover with tin foil and bake in a 375° F. (190° C.) oven for 30 minutes.

HARLEQUIN
PREMIERE AUTHOR EDITIONS

6 top Harlequin authors—6 of their best books!

1. **JANET DAILEY** Giant of Mesabi
2. **CHARLOTTE LAMB** Dark Master
3. **ROBERTA LEIGH** Heart of the Lion
4. **ANNE MATHER** Legacy of the Past
5. **ANNE WEALE** Stowaway
6. **VIOLET WINSPEAR** The Burning Sands

Harlequin is proud to offer these 6 exciting romance novels by
6 of our most popular authors. In brand-new beautifully
designed covers, each Harlequin Premiere Author Edition
is a bestselling love story—a contemporary, compelling and
passionate read to remember!

Available wherever paperback books are sold, or through
Harlequin Reader Service. Simply complete and mail the coupon below.

Harlequin Reader Service

In the U.S.
P.O. Box 52040
Phoenix, Ariz., 85072-9988

In Canada
649 Ontario Street
Stratford, Ontario N5A 6W2

Please send me the following editions of **Harlequin Premiere Author Editions**.
I am enclosing my check or money order for $1.95 for each copy ordered,
plus 75¢ to cover postage and handling.

☐ 1   ☐ 2   ☐ 3   ☐ 4   ☐ 5   ☐ 6

Number of books checked_____ @ $1.95 each = $_____

N.Y. state and Ariz. residents add appropriate sales tax $_____

Postage and handling $_____.75

I enclose $_____   TOTAL $_____
(Please send check or money order. We cannot be responsible for cash sent
through the mail.) Price subject to change without notice.

NAME_____
                              (Please Print)
ADDRESS_____ APT. NO._____

CITY_____

STATE/PROV._____ ZIP/POSTAL CODE_____

Offer expires April 30, 1984   31056000000

PA-W

Take these
4 best-selling novels
FREE

as advertised on TV

Yes! Four sophisticated, contemporary love stories by four world-famous authors of romance FREE, as your introduction to the Harlequin Presents subscription plan. Thrill to **Anne Mather**'s passionate story BORN OUT OF LOVE, set in the Caribbean.... Travel to darkest Africa in **Violet Winspear**'s TIME OF THE TEMPTRESS ....Let **Charlotte Lamb** take you to the fascinating world of London's Fleet Street in MAN'S WORLD .... Discover beautiful Greece in **Sally Wentworth**'s moving romance SAY HELLO TO YESTERDAY.

Harlequin Presents...

The very finest in romance fiction

Join the millions of avid Harlequin readers all over the world who delight in the magic of a really exciting novel. EIGHT great NEW titles published EACH MONTH! Each month you will get to know exciting, interesting, true-to-life people .... You'll be swept to distant lands you've dreamed of visiting .... Intrigue, adventure, romance, and the destiny of many lives will thrill you through each Harlequin Presents novel.

Get all the latest books before they're sold out!
As a Harlequin subscriber you actually receive your personal copies of the latest Presents novels immediately after they come off the press, so you're sure of getting all 8 each month.

Cancel your subscription whenever you wish!
You don't have to buy any minimum number of books. Whenever you decide to stop your subscription just let us know and we'll cancel all further shipments.

Your FREE gift includes

Anne Mather—Born out of Love
Violet Winspear—Time of the Temptress
Charlotte Lamb—Man's World
Sally Wentworth—Say Hello to Yesterday

FREE Gift Certificate
and subscription reservation

Mail this coupon today!

Harlequin Reader Service

In the U.S.A.
1440 South Priest Drive
Tempe, AZ 85281

In Canada
649 Ontario Street
Stratford, Ontario N5A 6W2

Please send me my 4 Harlequin Presents books free. Also, reserve a subscription to the 8 new Harlequin Presents novels published each month. Each month I will receive 8 new Presents novels at the low price of $1.75 each [*Total— $14.00 a month*]. There are no shipping and handling or any other hidden charges. I am free to cancel at any time, but even if I do, these first 4 books are still mine to keep absolutely FREE without any obligation. 108 BPP CAAK

Offer expires April 30, 1984

NAME	(PLEASE PRINT)
ADDRESS	APT. NO.
CITY	
STATE/PROV.	ZIP/POSTAL CODE

If price changes are necessary you will be notified.

Harlequin Presents

ALL-TIME FAVORITE BESTSELLERS
...love stories that grow more beautiful with time!

Now's your chance to discover the earlier great books in Harlequin Presents, the world's most popular romance-fiction series.

Choose from the following list.

ALL-TIME FAVORITE BESTSELLERS

Complete and mail this coupon today!

Harlequin Reader Service

In the U.S.A.
P.O. Box 52040
Phoenix, Arizona 85072-9988

In Canada
649 Ontario Street
Stratford, Ontario N5A 6W2

Please send me the following Presents **ALL-TIME FAVORITE BESTSELLERS.** I am enclosing my check or money order for $1.75 for each copy ordered, plus 75¢ to cover postage and handling.

☐ #17	☐ #38	☐ #50	☐ #67	☐ #75
☐ #20	☐ #41	☐ #54	☐ #70	☐ #78
☐ #32	☐ #42	☐ #62	☐ #71	☐ #83
☐ #35	☐ #46	☐ #66	☐ #73	

Number of copies checked @ $1.75 each = $ _____
N.Y. and Ariz. residents add appropriate sales tax $ _____
Postage and handling $ .75
                                            TOTAL $ _____

I enclose _____
(Please send check or money order. We cannot be responsible for cash sent through the mail.)
Prices subject to change without notice.

NAME _____
(Please Print)

ADDRESS _____ APT. NO. _____

CITY _____

STATE/PROV. _____

ZIP/POSTAL CODE _____

Offer expires April 30, 1984   31056000000

A Harlequin
ROBERTA LEIGH
Collector's Edition

A specially designed collection of six exciting love stories by one of the world's favorite romance writers—Roberta Leigh, author of more than 60 bestselling novels!

1 **Love in Store**
2 **Night of Love**
3 **Flower of the Desert**
4 **The Savage Aristocrat**
5 **The Facts of Love**
6 **Too Young to Love**

Available now wherever paperback books are sold, or available through Harlequin Reader Service. Simply complete and mail the coupon below.

Harlequin Reader Service

In the U.S.
P.O. Box 52040
Phoenix, AZ 85072-9988

In Canada
649 Ontario Street
Stratford, Ontario N5A 6W2

Please send me the following editions of the Harlequin Roberta Leigh Collector's Editions. I am enclosing my check or money order for $1.95 for each copy ordered, plus 75¢ to cover postage and handling.

☐ 1   ☐ 2   ☐ 3   ☐ 4   ☐ 5   ☐ 6

Number of books checked_____ @ $1.95 each = $_____

N.Y. state and Ariz. residents add appropriate sales tax $_____

Postage and handling $ .75

                                              TOTAL $_____

I enclose_____

(Please send check or money order. We cannot be responsible for cash sent through the mail.) Price subject to change without notice.

NAME_____
(Please Print)
ADDRESS_____ APT. NO._____

CITY_____

STATE/PROV._____ ZIP/POSTAL CODE_____

Offer expires April 30, 1984   31056000000

RL-N

ANNE MATHER

The world-renowned author of more than 90 great romances, including the runaway bestseller *Stormspell*, continues her triumph with...

WILD CONCERTO

Her second blockbuster romance!
Big exciting trade-size paperback!

A bizarre twist of fate thrusts the innocent Lani into the arms of a man she must never love. He is Jake Pendragon, a brilliant concert pianist romantically involved with a beautiful international opera star— who just happens to be Lani's mother!

A searing story of love and heartbreak, passion and revenge.

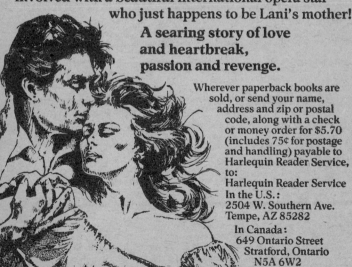

Wherever paperback books are sold, or send your name, address and zip or postal code, along with a check or money order for $5.70 (includes 75¢ for postage and handling) payable to Harlequin Reader Service, to:

Harlequin Reader Service
In the U.S.:
2504 W. Southern Ave.
Tempe, AZ 85282

In Canada:
649 Ontario Street
Stratford, Ontario
N5A 6W2

WC-N